A COWGIRL'S HEART

BARRELS AND HEARTS BOOK 2

EDITH MACKENZIE

My cowgirl heart was captured long ago by my own cowboy. Love you xx

*D*el cautiously sipped the ginger beer, hopeful it would ease the nausea that threatened to storm her esophagus and purge the contents of her stomach. It was getting beyond a joke. She hadn't managed to keep a full meal down for days now. At first, she put it down to the dodgy servo hotdog she had eaten, but now she was seriously starting to consider that she might have a medical condition on her hands.

There was only one thing left for a crook girl to do—consult Doctor Google. Typing in her symptoms, she took another careful sip. So far, so good. *Okay, here we go,* she thought as her screen filled with results. Anxiety, poor diet and dehydration, lupus, bowel cancer, irritable bowel syndrome. Geeze, she was seriously ill!

"Are you okay, Deb?" Frankie shifted uneasily in her chair. "You look a little queasy."

"Actually, she looks flat out like a lizard drinking," Megan griped. "When you're ready, dishes need to be done and it's your turn."

"Why is she giving a lizard a drink?" Gabi scrunched her

face up in confusion. "I didn't even know she had a pet lizard."

"It just means she's not that busy," Frankie explained. "I'll do the dishes before I head home. But I'm only doing it because you look awful, Deb. Aren't you feeling better yet?"

"I don't think I ever will, unless I can beat cancer," Deb muttered under her breath.

"What?" Frankie raised her chin in question.

"Never mind. Just talking to myself."

Megan perched herself on the arm of the sofa. "Guess who I saw this morning at the feed store?"

"Don't care, I'm dying here." Deb put her phone down as she accepted the inevitability of her prognosis.

"You're such a party pooper sometimes, Deb. But I'm going to ignore you." Megan stuck out her tongue. "I saw Mitch. And that's not all. I invited him to see the ranch tomorrow."

Frankie dried her hands on a towel. "I'm going to leave these dishes to drain and head home. Luciano will be home soon, and I don't want him getting lonely, if you know what I mean." Frankie winked smugly at the girls.

Deb thought she looked disgustingly happy. A wave of nausea forced her to close her eyes as she battled through it. Opening her eyes again once it passed, she locked them squarely with her friend. "Awesome, Megan," she said sarcastically. "Just awesome. And now, if you'll excuse me, I'm going to be sick."

The tailgate of the trailer gave a satisfying thump as it settled into place. Deb fumbled for the latch, trying to ignore the queasiness that was always just below the surface these days.

"We're only away for a few days this time. But I'll be flying out to see Luc in Jacksonville, so Gabi will bring the horses back." Frankie secured her side. Seeing Deb's pained expression, the look on her face grew concerned. "Are you still feeling crook?"

"Yeah, just have a really bad tummy bug I can't seem to shake."

"Deb, it's not normal to feel this lousy for so long. You need to go get yourself checked out," Frankie instructed firmly, her face stern. "Promise me you'll go if it gets too bad."

"Aye aye, boss," Deb touched her fingers to the brim of her hat in mocking salute.

"Is she being a pain again?" Megan said, emerging from the barn.

"Yes," the friends both replied simultaneously.

Megan laughed at her friends' equally comical expressions as each looked at each other accusingly, "I actually meant you, Deb." Her eyes hardened as they glared at Deb, "Just go to the doctors already. The sooner you get better, the sooner I won't have to cover you around the ranch."

"Geeze, if it will get everyone off my case, I'll think about it." Deb scuffed her boot in the dirt like a child who had just been told they had to go to the dentist.

Frankie rolled her eyes, looking skyward as if seeking divine guidance. Finding none, she shook her head, clearly not willing to admit defeat. "Megan, if she changes her mind, can you please make her?" Exasperation laced her voice.

"I'm not a child," Deb protested.

"Then don't act like one," Gabi commented, stowing her gear bag into the back of the truck.

Deb screwed up her face and crossed her eyes at her. Frankie threw her hands up in defeat. "I give up. Die then. Just do it quietly."

"And preferably after you've helped with the horses so I don't get stuck with all the work. Again," Megan added sourly.

"Well, that's our cue to hit the road. Any problems, give us a call or get Papai to sort it," Gabi instructed. "Is the new farrier coming out today?"

"That's right, Mitch is coming today, isn't he?" Frankie said.

"Haven't you noticed how good a mood Megan is in?" Deb said sarcastically. Given the fact that her friend was notorious for being territorial where Mitch was concerned, she was not looking forward to the visit. It was a bit odd since, out of all of them, Deb had known him the longest and therefore should be the most possessive of his time. Guess she just didn't roll like that.

"Say 'hello' for me, and I'll catch up with him next time." Frankie settled herself in the car.

"Will do." In a flash, Megan's mood switched, and she swatted Deb playfully on the bum. "Now, get to work."

Deb watched in amusement as Megan bolted into the bathroom in a fresh change of clothes. Deciding she should probably check her own cleanliness, she lifted her arm and gave her pit a quick sniff. The rank smell of musty body odor assailed her nostrils, her nose wrinkling in protest. Maybe a quick dose of deodorant wouldn't be out of place, she mused. While she was at it, she should probably brush her teeth. Frequent reflux had left her mouth tasting like a small animal had crawled inside and died, not to mention the residual fuzzy feeling on her teeth. At the least, she should definitely be chewing some gum. Thankfully, the nausea had settled down as she worked, the fresh air lifting her spirits.

After cleaning herself up, she left Megan to her last-minute grooming and headed down to Sampson's stall. Being a young and inquisitive creature as Frankie so generously described him, his latest trick was to flip his feed bucket around his stall, flinging his feed about in the process. Well, Deb had finally had enough. She was going to fix his wagon and install a feeder mounted to the stall wall. If she could successfully complete the project, she would begin implementing them to the other stalls and hopefully cut down on feed wastage. Gabi would certainly be pleased. In her mind's eye, Deb could see her friend's rapt expression as she fastidiously entered the savings into her spreadsheets.

Finding her cordless drill and some screws, she sat down on an upturned bucket as she read the instructions on the box. A wave of nausea washed over her, clogging her throat. Sweat beaded on her forehead as she tried to breathe deeply, praying it would pass. Her stomach began to clench, painfully giving notice that evacuation of its contents was imminent. Stumbling to her feet, she clasped her hand tightly to her mouth. Desperately seeking the bathroom, she bolted blindly toward the bunkhouse. The acid clawed at her throat. She tried to force down the bile, but it was too late. Losing the battle at the base of the stairs, coughing and choking, she heaved her breakfast up in a great splashing geyser. Her stomach kept contracting, violently forcing everything up and out.

"What the bloody heck, Deb?" exclaimed Megan, appalled at the spectacle laid out before her.

Her face white and dripping bile, sweat, and tears, Deb miserably opened her eyes, suddenly aware that Mitch had just been about to step off the stairs. To her horror, his perfectly polished boots were now sporting a splatter design, collateral damage to her projectile vomit.

Face blanched, she forced herself to raise her eyes. "Hey Mitch, long time."

Mitch looked down at his boots. "I'd like to be able to say that's the first bloody time that's ever happened to me." He gave a wry smile. "But I reckon I can't. You feeling all right, Deb?"

Feeling the warning burn in her throat again, Deb pushed past Megan and Mitch and scrambled to the safety of the bathroom. She heard Megan's outraged 'Excuse you', and lurched forward, sinking to her knees on the cold bathroom tiles beside the toilet, and vomited until only clear liquid remained. The pungent stench invaded her nostrils and she heaved even though there was nothing left.

She curled up in the fetal position, the chill of the hard floor a soothing balm to her fevered cheek where it made contact. Hot tears spilled from her eyes leaving long, wet trails across her face, dripping relentlessly onto the smooth tile. Deb closed her eyes and gave into the bottomless misery that engulfed her, unable to fight its pull any longer.

CHAPTER 2

She would be brave, Deb decided as she flicked through the out-of-date magazine, stoic in her acceptance of whatever disease the doctor diagnosed her with. A toddler, screaming like a banshee, picked up a toy telephone and proceeded to use it as a makeshift shank to attack her mother's knee.

"Now, honey, Mommy doesn't like that." The under-attack parent attempted to placate the terrible creature. Deb was impressed with the woman's restraint, if not her parenting skills, as undeterred said honey doubled down on its violence.

"Deborah Burke?"

Deb quickly put her magazine down and followed the expectantly waiting doctor into the calm of his examination room. Looking toward the computer screen, the doctor pulled up her records before turning enquiring eyes at her. "What seems to be the problem today?"

"I haven't been very well lately, um, Doctor..." She scanned his name badge. "Fahdge? Ah, am I pronouncing that right?"

"Yes, as in fudge," he responded with a long-suffering

expression. "You have no idea how much fun they had with that at Medical School."

"I can imagine. It's sweet, makes me all gooey and, at the same time, want caramel."

"Are you done?" the good doctor asked patiently.

"For now. But I reserve the right to continue this line of conversation at any time during this appointment. Especially if I get bad news."

A faint smile ghosted Dr Fahdge's lips. "Of course. Now, can you be more specific about your ailments?"

"I feel like I want to chuck up all of the time. Bloody real crook, you know? First, I thought it was from a dodgy servo hot dog, but it lasted way longer than that. I'm bloody tired all of the time. I mean, I work on a ranch with horses, I'm always kinda tired. But this is next level. By the arvo, I'm rooted, and just want to put on my tracky dacks and veg." Pursing her lips, she paused, mentally ticking off her symptoms. "Oh, and I need to pee a lot. But that could be because I'm drinking a lot more to get rid of the metallic taste that's always in my mouth. I haven't felt like that since I tested a 9-volt battery on my tongue."

Doctor Fahdge's expression was somewhat dazed by the time her diatribe ceased. Blinking a couple of times, he cleared his throat. "To be clear, you are experiencing nausea, fatigue, a more frequent need to urinate, and a metallic taste in your mouth?"

Deb nodded sharply. "Yep, that's what I just bloody said." She shuffled a little in her chair. "So, how serious is it?"

"I will need to ask a few more questions. I always like to remove the possibility of minor reasons first. When did you last have your period?"

"Ages ago, like, years. I have hyperthyroidism, so..." She trailed off, giving a dismissive shrug.

"Is there a possibility that you might be pregnant?"

Deb laughed, shaking her head in amusement. "You'd

have to have sex for that!" A thought snaked its way into her consciousness, leaving a cold trail of dread in its wake. "Oh, wait, there was this one time recently."

"I've heard that's all it takes." A hint of humor snuck past Dr Fahdge's professional façade. "Would you like me to get a test for you to check?" The doctor asked gently, clearly taking in her bemused state. "It's the same as the store-bought ones. Urinate on it, and in a few minutes, it will give a result." At her little nod of acknowledgement, he reached into his drawer for a kit. "Depending on this, I will order more tests to confirm. The bathroom is down the hall on the right. Once you are done, can you please give the result to a nurse and she will book you in for another appointment."

The two thin lines leapt off the kit, the starkness of the indigo contrasting sharply against the white background. The rest of the world faded to nonexistence, and Deb's hand began to tremble at the proof she held within her grasp, her mind struggling to fathom what her eyes saw. A hysterical giggle bubbled up at the absurdity of her situation. *Trust me to get a faulty kit.* She giggled to herself in denial. Sitting in the doctor surgery's cold, lonely bathroom, the harsh reality of the situation hit home. Her tears of mirth turned to those of uncertainty and fear.

Holy crap, what do I do now?

It was a small blessing to find Megan gone when she returned to the bunkhouse. Emotionally drained, Deb had only enough strength remaining to climb into bed and pull the covers under her chin. Old memories tugged her back to her childhood where, once again, she was little and scared of the vastness of the dark. Her mum used to tuck her into a cozy nest of covers and pillows, the whisper of her lips on her forehead as she kissed her goodnight. The shadows would dissolve into normal nighttime darkness, and she would drift off to sleep, certain in the knowledge that in the morning, all would be well with the world. That she was safe. Gosh, how she longed for it all to be so simple now. Silent tears tracked down her cheeks as her misery spilled from her.

The forlorn silence of the room was broken by the harsh beep of her phone. Fumbling to pick it up she saw an unfamiliar number illuminated on the screen.

Hey, It's Mitch. Megan gave me your number. You okay?

She rubbed her eyes, suddenly no longer feeling alone. At a loss to how on earth she could respond to a message like that, she threw her phone back on her bedside table. She flopped onto her back to stare at the ceiling, wondering if she was ever going to be okay again.

CHAPTER 3

The next few days rolled by with Deb manically attempting to keep herself busy. It marginally helped that, since her doctor's appointment, it was as if a magical switch had been flicked, vanquishing her nausea to the dim realm of memory. Her brain overloaded and unable to process the concept of being pregnant, she safely tucked the information far away in her mind least the feeling of terrified helplessness overwhelmed her completely. Flying under the radar had proven to be surprisingly easy. With Frankie and Gabi away as usual and Megan caught up with Mitch being back on the scene, none were the wiser about her little doctor's appointment.

Exhaustion rolled over her like a thick fog. Giving into the lassitude, she leaned on the stable fork, resting her chin on top as she closed her eyes.

"Oh, hi, Mitch." Megan's voice drifted from further up the barn. Deb imagined Megan flicking her hair back as she spoke. "What can I do for you?"

"Hey, Megan. Is Deb around?"

The silence was deafening. "Deb?"

"Yeah, I sent her a message the other night to see if she

was okay and I haven't heard back. Thought I'd better check in on her and make sure she hasn't carked it yet."

"I can confirm she is still alive, so you can stop worrying about her." A sharp edge cut through Megan's voice like razor blades. "How did your boots clean up, by the way?"

Deb peeked out from the stall to guiltily gauge his reaction. "Nothing I couldn't handle," he responded, giving Megan a wary look. "Is there something I'm missing here?"

"I don't follow."

"You seem a little mad at me," he said tentatively.

"Mad?" Megan laughed—a little too brightly to Deb's ear. "No," she said dismissively, waving his suggestion away. "But if you're worried about it, you can always buy me dinner." She smiled coyly up at him.

"Sure, let's get Deb and grab something to eat," he suggested, giving Megan a direct look.

Megan looked hurt. "Deb might not want to go."

"Why don't we ask her?" he countered.

Deb stood rooted to the spot, her eyes frantically searching for an escape.

"Deb, do you want to go to dinner with Mitch and I?"

Knowing the gig was up, she gave a soft little sigh before poking her head fully out of the stall. "I might pass tonight. I'm feeling a bit knackered."

"That's okay. I can take a raincheck until you feel better," he said, oblivious to the frozen smile on Megan's face. "Are you feeling better? You look better than last time."

Surprised the man was still standing given the daggers Megan was shooting his way, Deb stepped from the stall. "I haven't vomited for days."

"My boots are bloody relieved," he said, giving her a wink. "Well, I'd better leave you girls to it. I'm glad you're not crook anymore."

Deb stood awkwardly, watching as Megan said goodbye. Once he had left, Megan held up her hand to halt whatever she thought Deb was going to say. "I don't want to hear it," she said icily and marched off to the bunkhouse. Deb heaved a sigh. *Great.*

Ironically, although Frankie had flown to spend a few days with Luciano, by the time Gabi drove the horses home, they both arrived a few hours apart. Deb didn't care who got home first. She was just eternally grateful to have someone to break up the constant onslaught of dirty looks she was on the receiving end of. She tried to talk rationally with Megan, that her and Mitch had been friends since they were in kindy, but it did nothing to soften her demeanor. If only she knew just how little chasing a man factored on her radar right now.

Deb was lucid enough to know she would eventually have to tackle the pregnancy and figure out a game plan. But for now, she was doing her best to put one foot in front of the other and keep moving. If she stood still too long, a suffocating fear threatened to smother her. She felt better if she continued to be her usual capable self, even if it was now only a brittle façade in danger of splintering.

Frankie appeared refreshed, her eyes sparkling vibrantly as she strode into the barn, blonde ponytail bouncing with each step. It was through a supreme effort of self-control that Deb didn't throw a ball of horse manure at her. Frankie, unaware of how close she was to suffering a poo-castrophe, breezily waltzed over to Deb.

"Hey, you look better."

Remorse for her earlier unkind thoughts made her shuffle her feet. "Yeah, I am."

"Megan said you went to the doctors. But only after you vomited all over poor Mitch's boots." Frankie laughed delightedly at the image. "I miss out on all of the good stuff."

"Yeah, well Megan can talk about poor Mitch," Deb muttered sourly, resentment at her friend's unfair treatment making her hackles raise.

"I wish I'd been here to see Mitch's face." Gabi chortled, both girls still not picking up on Deb's hostility.

Embarrassed tears filled Deb's eyes, catching her by surprise. She dashed them away angrily, ducking her head to hide the movement. Frankie's eyes opened wide in horror. "Oh, crap. Are you crying, Deb?"

Gabi looked remorseful. "I'm sorry, I was only teasing."

Frankie hugged Deb. "Yeah, I'm sorry. I didn't mean anything by it. Are you really okay?"

Deb sniffled, suspecting she may have overreacted to their banter. "It's just that Megan's been a real cow about the Mitch thing ever since it happened."

"How about we go upstairs and get a cup of coffee? You can tell us all about it." Frankie started to lead her friend toward the bunkhouse stairs.

Deb followed meekly, feeling guilty about her earlier mutinous thoughts toward her happy friend. Her emotions sure were giving her one bloody heck of a ride lately. Gabi put the kettle on, and Frankie got the mugs out of the overhead cupboard. Deb awkwardly washed her hands in an attempt to distract herself from her thoughts. Giving up, she flopped down.

"No coffee for me, thanks. I'll just have an OJ," Deb said softly from the kitchen table. Frankie, reaching for a mug, paused mid-stretch and shot Gabi a mystified look. Both girls turned to give Deb their full attention.

"Okay, what's really going on? Who are you, and what have you done with Deb?" Frankie demanded.

"Very funny," Deb said. "I just don't feel like coffee." She folded her arms defensively across her chest.

Frankie walked slowly to the table, her gaze steady. "I've known you for a long time, Deb. Most days, you have more coffee in your blood system than blood." Frankie slumped into the chair. "You're dying, aren't you?" she wailed.

"You should have told us," accused Gabi as she began to cry, too. "We would have come back as soon as we found out."

"Should you even be out of bed?" Not waiting for a reply, Frankie stood abruptly. "You should be in bed."

"I'll call your doctors. I need to understand your treatment schedule so I can take care of the appointments," Gabi said, appearing to take comfort from taking charge of the situation.

Pure love for her friends filled Deb to her very core and her throat tightened as unshed tears burned her eyes. "I'm not dying, guys."

Frankie collapsed back on her chair with a thump. "Then what is it? And don't tell me nothing, there is obviously something going on."

Deb looked down at her hands as her fingers knotted themselves together. "I, um…" She cleared her throat. "It appears I'm pregnant."

The complete absence of sound was deafening as stunned silence filled the room. Her friends' reactions verged on comical. Gabi blinked rapidly several times while Frankie opened and closed her mouth, robbed of speech. Finally, gathering her scattered wits, Frankie swallowed loudly.

"Say what?"

"I'm pregnant." Deb was amazed at how calm her voice sounded. Inside, she was a quivering mess.

"Gosh. I mean, how? I mean, I know how, but you know what I mean," Frankie spluttered.

Deb's face grew serious. "Well Frankie, when a man and a woman love each other very much… Honestly, I'm surprised Luciano hasn't explained it to you by now."

Comprehension blossomed on Gabi's face, her eyes as wide as saucers. "It was the night we went to the bar." She turned to Frankie. "When you were broken up with Luciano." She turned back to Deb. "I'm right, aren't I?"

Deb was saved from having to answer. "What's going on?" Megan asked, stamping through the door.

"Get your butt in here and stop being mean to Deb," Frankie commanded in a voice that brooked no disobedience. She pointed to a vacant chair.

Megan had the grace to look sheepish. "Yeah, well."

"Let it go, Megan," Frankie warned. "Deb needs us right now."

Looking at the myriad of expressions around the table, Megan grudgingly sat down. "Okay, bring me up to speed."

Frankie looked toward Deb for permission. At her nod, she continued. "Deb's pregnant. It was from the night at the bar and we are all about to find out the name of the father." She turned back to Deb, waiting expectantly, her hands clasped in front of her in anticipation.

"Tucker Brown." Blank stares greeted her announcement. Frankie glanced at Megan with furrowed brows. Megan shrugged.

"How do we contact this Tucker Brown?" Gabi asked.

"I don't really have any contacts for him," Deb murmured softly, shame painting her cheeks crimson. "It's not like I was planning on seeing him ever again." Miserable tears flowed down her face, no longer able to hide from the reality of her situation.

Her friends shot each other horrified looks around the table, Frankie jumped up and wrapped her arms fiercely around Deb. "I'm sure we can figure it out. You're not going to do this alone, you hear me? You have us."

Megan shuffled over and joined them. "Sorry for being such a troll, but you know I love you. Thank God the kid is going to have Auntie Megan to show it how to be cool."

Gabi was the only one not in on the hugfest, busily

tapping away on her phone. "Give me an hour and I'll find him, Deb," she promised.

～

"Found him!" Gabi crowed triumphantly, waving her phone about in the air.

The girls scampered over, eager to see the father-to-be. All except Deb. Her feet were suddenly pure lead, immovable lumps of flesh held fast to the floor. It was as if she watched it all transpire from afar. Frankie looking down at the phone, a look of abject horror crossing her pinched features as she looked up.

"Please tell me this isn't him," she said.

Gabi and Megan looked between the two of them in confusion. Gabi's brows drew together as she shrugged. "This might not be him. I need Deb to check first." She gave Frankie a piercing look. "What on earth is the matter with you Frankie?" she asked in exasperation. "You look like you've seen a ghost!"

"I'd be so lucky for him to be a ghost and not still breathing," Frankie muttered disgustedly.

"Okay, can someone tell me what's going on?" asked a wide-eyed Megan. "I thought this was about Deb. But somehow this is now about Frankie. I'm confused."

"You and me both," said Deb, finally rising from her stupor to stride over and snatch the phone from Frankie's hand. "Yep, that's him." Hands planted on her hips, she glared suspiciously at Frankie. "What's the bloody big deal?"

Frankie wrung her hands together. "You're sure that's him? Like, really, really sure? I mean you could be confused, and he just kinda looks like the father?" She wrinkled her nose, "Please tell me he's not the father."

Deb looked back down at the picture on the screen. The hair was the exact same shade of blond, the lip curl like she remembered. "I know I had a fair bit to drink that night, but I'm telling you that's bloody him." She handed the phone back. "Now, spill."

Fingers still tightly entwined, Frankie refused to accept the phone, she wet her lips nervously. "That's the arse-grabbing bronc rider. You know, the one Luciano beat the snot out of?"

"Strewth," muttered Megan.

"Strewth all right. Have another look," Gabi commanded, pushing Deb's hand with the phone back up to her face.

Deb shrugged her off and crossed her arms defiantly across her chest. "I don't need to. That's bloody him."

Frankie swallowed hard. "Okay then. What do you want to do next?"

Deb glanced down at her hands, still warm from the heat of the phone. "Honestly? Go into my room and pretend none of this is happening."

Frankie covered Deb's hand with her own and gave it a sympathetic squeeze. "Honey, I can't even begin to say I know how you're feeling right now. But no matter what, we're all here for you. You do what you need to do, and we'll support you in your decision."

Deb looked around at the loving, supportive faces of her friends. "I guess I need to put my big girl pants on and tell him." Frankie smiled at her gently as she gave Deb's hand another squeeze. Wordlessly, Deb stood, a wan smile on her face, and strode toward her bedroom.

It was only when she had safely closed the door on her friends that she allowed her shoulders to slump, no longer able to carry the weight of her forced bravado. She retrieved her phone and punched his name into the search bar. Sure enough, his face appeared. She tapped the message icon, her breath accelerating as black spots danced before her eyes. Trying to subdue the anxiety that threatened to gain control, she buried her face in her hands and attempted to breathe. *How the bloody heck had she gotten into this mess?*

She gave a final sniff as she straightened, typing determinedly. Afraid her courage would desert her, she quickly pressed send. Drained, and the last of her resolve ebbing away, she flopped back on her bed and cried.

CHAPTER 4

The two new broodmares flicked their heads as they frolicked in the quarantine paddock. Having arrived that morning, they were still unsettled, nervous tension evident in each gesture as they performed their delicate dance to gauge the other's dominance. A lifetime of being around horses, and their raw power and majesty still entranced Deb. She watched, envious of the spirited freedom they displayed. Their joyous liberty only served to heighten her sense of being wretchedly trapped. Heaving a sigh, she took one last covetous glance at the playful mares and pushed herself off the fence rail.

Breaking an earlier promise to herself, she pulled her phone from the pocket of her jeans and looked at the message.

Don't remember you. I go through lots of girls. Your problem, not mine. Keep it. Get rid of it. Don't care.

Deb's eyes burned with humiliation, the hurt of being dismissed as easily as one would throw away trash stung.

"Deb, the mares look to be in fine form today. Gabriella will be happy to see them settled in so well when she gets home tomorrow," called Senhor Eduardo as he strode purposely toward her.

Quickly, she rubbed the tears from her eyes. "They will be happy here," she agreed.

He looked closely at her face, clearly noting her red eyes, and his face crinkled with concern. "Are you all right? You are not hurt?"

Deb gave a little sniff. How did she answer that? Right now, there seemed to be no end to the tormenting gloom that hovered over her. "I'm, um, yeah. Getting there, I guess." And then she cried. Senhor Eduardo took one alarmed look at her and pulled her into a rough hug.

"I don't know what is the matter, but Sra Ana always makes things better with some coffee. Let's find her."

Deb, embarrassed at crying in front of him, gave a little nod as he gently escorted her to the main house.

"Ana," he called as he approached. Sra Ana took one look at the distraught girl's face and bustled her husband into the house with firm instructions to bring back a pot of coffee and some fresh cookies. She took Deb's hand and guided her to one of the porch chairs.

"Would you like to talk about it?" she asked kindly.

"I guess. Everyone will know soon enough." She paused, remorse filling her at her ungrateful tone. "I'm sorry, Sra Ana. I've just had a lot on my mind. I don't even know where to bloody begin." Sra Ana gave her an encouraging smile. "I guess I will just say it. I'm pregnant." Senhor Eduardo, who had just stepped out on the porch, put the pot down with a clatter. Sra Ana's mouth was open in shock. "I understand if you don't want me to stay here anymore, now that I'm pregnant. I just need a bit of time to find a new place and—" The tears burst through her determined wall to contain them and spilled freely down her face. "And I'm sorry for crying. I've been doing that a lot lately, and I never cry. I'm the one that's capable. Frankie's the crier," she wailed.

Sra Ana gently seated herself on the armrest of Deb's chair and wrapped her arms around the sobbing girl. "Ah, child, you misunderstand me. I am shocked, yes. But never would I—we—turn you out," she said, looking over Deb's head to Senhor Eduardo for agreement.

He nodded. "Your home is here with us, and so is the baby's. I look forward to being an avo, a grandfather."

"Gabriella does not look like she will give me one anytime soon. I cannot wait to meet my adoptive grandbaby," Sra Ana said, her eyes misty.

"The father, does he know?" Senhor Eduardo asked gently.

Deb looked down at her hands in embarrassment. "He does. And he doesn't want anything to do with us."

"Then that is his loss," Senhor Eduardo said fiercely. "This baby will want for nothing."

Deb looked at the Brazilian couple in gratitude, humbled by their support. Those dang tears threatened once again. "Thank you."

"Now, what have you been eating?" Sra demanded, suddenly all business. Deb smiled through her tears at the similarity in manner with her no-nonsense daughter.

The steady clip clop of horses' hooves hitting the packed earth kept steady time with Deb's own strides. These were the last two that needed to be brought in, and then she could take a break and rest her swollen feet. Mitch was due shortly to trim the broodmares' hooves, but Megan had quickly claimed the task of holding them. Not that Deb cared much, not when a nice comfy chair had her name all over it. Turning the corner to the barn, she spied Mitch's truck already parked and the steady rasp of file on hoof coming from inside.

Leading her charges in, she spied Megan at Delila's head chatting animatedly to the bent form of the farrier. She quietly guided her mares past, careful not to disturb the golden mare, and placed them in a couple of free stalls. Time for that packet of Tim Tams she had stashed away waiting for an opportunity for her to eat, free from her friends and having to share with them.

"Hey, Deb," Mitch said, his voice muffled from his bowed position.

"Oh, hi, Mitch. How you been?" She slowed her steps to stand beside Megan.

"Busy. Been getting lots of referral work from the vets and owners of horses Frankie's trained."

"No rest for the wicked." Megan winked suggestively at him.

Mitch laughed, the low rumble making Deb smile in return. "Strewth, I don't reckon I've been that bloody bad."

"A girl can dream," countered Megan, giving him a coy smile.

Mitch smiled awkwardly, shifting his gaze to Deb. "So, um, are you still feeling better?"

A broad grin broke out over her face. "I am. Your boots are safe. They still have nothing to fear from me."

"That's good to know. Do you want to catch up for a drink sometime?"

Deb's mouth opened and closed. She could feel Megan's sharp look drilling into her. "Ah, I'm not really drinking much these days."

Mitch laughed haughtily, his eyes adorably crinkled. "Sure. Next you're going to tell me you've bloody given up coffee."

Megan gleamed with suppressed mirth at her friend's expense, clearly waiting to see how this line of conversation was going to play out. She was obviously not going to be any help.

"Um, yeah, I don't really do caffeine anymore," Deb fumbled, shifting her weight restlessly.

"Strewth. Whatever's wrong must be bloody serious," he teased.

"Life changing," agreed Megan, grinning spitefully.

Deb heaved a sigh. What was the point in keeping it quiet? She wasn't going to be able to hide it forever and it had been nice to tell the Cabreras. Well, once she'd stopped crying. "I'm pregnant."

Mitch burst out laughing again, looking from Megan to Deb, waiting for them to join him in the joke. His expression rapidly sobered when he realized no one else was joining him in the merriment. "Oh, crap. You're bloody serious."

"There are some things I need to do," Deb said stiffly, her cheeks hot. "Catch ya." She spun on her heels and dejection flooded her as she closed the bunkhouse door behind her. What had she been thinking? Of course this was funny to other people. Just a big joke. A gentle knock sounded on the door and, a second later, Mitch entered the room, a shamed expression on his face as he fiddled with the strap of his farrier chaps.

"Strewth, Deb, I'm sorry. I just, well, how was I to know you weren't bloody joking?" He twisted the strap tightly.

"Because that's something I would never blooming joke about. Do the chicks you know joke about that?" she demanded, her body rigid with outrage.

He spread his hands wide in peace. "You're right. I was just bloody shocked, I think. Well, I guess congratulations are in order. Is the father excited?" Deb made a choked sound, drawing a concerned, slightly wary look from Mitch. "He is happy, right?"

"He doesn't want anything to do with us."

"What kind of drongo doesn't want anything to do with his baby?" Mitch exploded.

Deb began to cry pitifully. "The type that doesn't care if I keep the baby or not."

Mitch's face crumpled. "Aww Deb, come here." He enveloped her in his embrace. The musky fragrance of sweat and horses surrounding her was oddly comforting. "I'm sorry he's such a tool. But you're not alone, okay?" Deb nodded sniffling. "Please don't cry anymore," he begged uselessly.

"I would, but all I seem to do these days is cry at the drop of a hat." Deb laughed through her tears. "I think it's all the hormones."

Brisk footsteps sounded up the stairs, causing Deb to pull out of the embrace, Mitch reluctantly allowing her. Sra Ana bustled in carrying a covered tray. She gave Mitch an assessing glance before setting it on the table. Deb's nose could make out hints of butter and fresh bread. Her mouth began to salivate. Sra Ana pulled the cloth back to reveal steaming warm buttered bread rolls and what looked to be some type of chicken soup.

"This will be better for you and the baby than those horrible black sandwiches you make."

"It's Vegemite," Deb corrected. "And quite high in B vitamins." Beside her, Mitch swallowed a laugh.

Sra Ana's look hardened to steel. "No more black sandwiches. You need balanced meals. Now sit. Eat."

Deb sat. She grabbed one of the buttered rolls and dunked it into the soup. "This is delicious. Thank you, Sra Ana."

Sra Ana focused her attention on Mitch. He attempted to look nonchalant, but more closely resembled a deer caught in the spotlight. "I believe you are the new farrier?"

"Yes, Ma'am," he replied. "I'm Mitch." He offered her his hand. After a moment's hesitation that appeared like she was judging his worth, she grudgingly accepted.

"That is right. I remember the girls saying you are an old Australian friend of theirs."

"Yes. I've known Deb the longest, but all of them for quite some time."

She gave him a leveled look. Mitch was the first to drop his eyes. Deb took another nibble of bread, enjoying the show. It wasn't everyday someone got Mitch on the back foot. "I believe there are still some horses that need to be done," Sra Ana noted expressionlessly.

"Yes, Ma'am. I'll leave you to your lunch, Deb," he said, obediently exiting the room.

Sra Ana, looking pleased with herself, gave Deb a smug wink before she left and Deb was alone. She wasn't sure what the heck had just happened, but Sra Ana did make one heck of a fine lunch.

CHAPTER 5

*L*anterns hung festively from the branches of the massive live oak tree. The table once again groaned under the weight of the food prepared by the deft hand of Sra Ana. Deb smiled as she watched Luciano twirl Frankie around as they danced, proudly celebrating his wife's success at gaining her Pro Card. Elsewhere, Gabi beamed with happiness as she spoke to her parents, relieved another hurdle had been removed in the rise of Affinity Stud Ranch. Megan joined Deb, sullenly handing her a glass of cool lemonade.

"Sra Ana gave me this with strict instructions that you're to drink it while it's nice and cold."

Deb guiltily snuck a glance at Sra Ana, feeling like a naughty child. She had been feeling a little flustered with the heat, but it was only as the cool soothing liquid slid down her throat that she realized how parched she was. "Thanks, Megan. I needed that," she said gratefully.

"Just following orders. Personally, I'm happy that I still have beer." Megan emphasized her point by chugging hers down.

"Are we cool, Megan?" Deb asked abruptly, tired of the

distance that had grown between them the last few days. "'Cause I'm over the attitude I've been copping from you lately."

Megan turned to face her, eyes narrowed angrily, tension radiating from tightly held body. "I get you're pregnant, okay? You're my friend, but do you have to take bloody everything? It was bad enough when it was Frankie. I'm used to being second behind her, but you?"

Deb jerked back in surprise at the venom in Megan's voice. "What the bloody heck?"

"It doesn't even matter. Mitch will be here soon. And then it will be poor pregnant Deb, and he's just eating that up, isn't he?" Before Deb could answer, Megan furiously strode away to join Gabi, leaving her standing there, catching flies with her mouth.

"Sorry I'm late, but better late than never, hey?" Mitch said from behind her. *Perfect timing.* Deb sighed as Megan glared at her from across the way.

She smiled. "It sure is," she said as she turned around to greet him. "I should probably introduce you to the others you haven't met yet."

Mitch looked down at the bag he held in his hands. "In a minute. I saw these in a shop window the other day and I thought of you," he said as he handed it to her.

Deb peered in curiously, unsure what to expect. A small bundle of tissue paper lay inside. She wrinkled her nose in uncertainty. "Should I be scared?"

"Nah, nothing like that," he assured her, looking a little like he was having second thoughts.

She pulled back the delicate paper to expose the tiniest pair of soft leather cowboy boots she had ever seen. Deb turned them over in her hands, marveling at the buttery softness of the tan suede. "I don't know what to say. They're beautiful," she said, humbled at his gift.

"I figured they aren't RM William's, but when in Rome

and all that, these were the next best thing. I'll need to keep an eye out for a little stock whip for the little tacker too."

Deb laughed. "Remember when we first learned how to crack a whip and you nearly took that old stock hand's eye out?"

"How was I supposed to know he was that bloody close? No good sneaking up on a bloke like that." He laughed.

"If I remember correctly, you were pretty good at sneaking yourself." Frankie joined in as she strolled contentedly over, hand in hand with Luciano.

It was impossible to look at the newly married couple and not see the love they had for each other radiating off them. Deb peeked at Mitch, curious to see his reaction to the pair. He seemed genuinely happy to see Frankie, but nothing untoward. Luciano quite clearly was sizing him up. Deb wondered how much he knew about Frankie and Mitch's shared history.

Frankie glanced down at the little cowboy booties Deb held, forgotten in her hands. "They're so cute." She gave her husband an adoring look. "But don't be getting any ideas. Not just yet," she teased. "Luc, this is our friend, Mitch. The old friend I told you about. Mitch, this is my husband, Luciano."

Luciano gave Mitch an appraising look as he extended his hand. "Frankie has told me a bit about you."

Mitch returned Luciano's handshake firmly. "Yes, well it's been good to catch up with the girls now that I'm here. Frankie seems bloody happy being married to you," he said as he released his grip. "I think I lost about a third of my body weight once she and the girls left."

Luciano chuckled as he patted his belly. "I think I gained it. I know I shouldn't eat all the desserts she makes, but how does a man stop?"

"It hasn't affected your riding. Looks like you're having another good year."

"I hope it will be. You are looking after the ranch's horses now? When you have a chance, I would like you to come out and look over mine."

"I can fit you in start of next week," Mitch suggested.

"That will work. What are you drinking? Beer?" Luciano asked, leading Mitch away from the girls.

Deb and Frankie exchanged an amused look. "I think they're going to be mates," Frankie whispered.

"Looks like it," agreed Deb, strangely pleased by the thought. Her smile froze as she caught Megan's dark look. *Apparently, we can't all be friends at the same time.*

"I've booked five of our mares to go to McGomery's stallion, so I will need one of you to haul them over in the next few months. Delila will obviously go to Sampson. That means I just need to find another stallion to put the two new mares to." Gabi glanced down at her laptop. "I think that's everything?"

Deb determinedly looked down at her mug. "So, what's the plan now I can't help with working horses?"

"Obviously, I will still train the horses when I'm here," began Frankie. "But Megan, do you think you will be able to continue what you've been doing and work them while I'm gone?" She looked at Megan to gauge her reaction.

"I don't like working strange horses all the time. I'm not a trainer like you, Frankie. But as long as I know that Deb will eventually be coming back to work the horses, then I don't have a problem."

"Good. Now that's all sorted, I think we can end this meeting and get to the real work." Frankie headed to the sink to rinse her coffee mug.

"Frankie, we've talked about this. Meetings are still

considered real work," Gabi said, following closely on her heels.

"I thought meetings were where you told us what you wanted us to do." Deb grabbed her hat as she headed for the door.

"Finally, something I can agree with you about." Megan followed suit.

"Good help is so hard to find," grumbled Gabi, throwing a dish cloth at them.

Both ducked, dodging her missile. Laughing, Deb wiggled her bum. "Especially with what you pay." With one final shimmy, she escaped out of range, her laughter fading away.

Gabi trotted behind her mother as Sra Ana carried the covered tray to the table. Obviously intrigued, she pulled the corner of the cloth up to peek at the bounty hidden underneath. Sharply, without sparing her daughter a single glance, Sra Ana slapped Gabi's hand away. "Not for you."

"But Mae, that smells like sopa de fuba." Gabi tugged at the cloth cover again. "Oww, that hurts," she protested as her mother slapped her hand again.

"When you give me a grandbaby, I will make you all the sopa de fuba you wish. Till then, not for you." Sra Ana gestured to Deb, who had watched the exchange from the safety of the couch, to come over.

If Deb's nose wasn't mistaken, there was some sort of sausage involved in this sopa da fuba, her stomach reminding her she hadn't eaten since breakfast. "It smells delicious, Sra Ana," Deb said as she seated herself down at the table. "What is it, exactly?"

Sra Ana whipped the cloth off, revealing a thick creamy yellow soup, bits of green flecked around the sausages that swam throughout. "This is sopa de fuba, a soup which is made with cornmeal, collard greens and sausages. There are a few other things, but that is my secret." Her eyes sparkled with pride. "And my Mae's before me."

"Yeah, it's only like, one of my favorite things ever." Gabi quickly snaffled a piece of sausage from the dish, ignoring her mother's warning look, and popped it into her mouth. "Yep, still good."

Deb brought a steaming spoonful to her mouth, the vapor leaving a little patch of condensation on her upper lip as she carefully blew on it before putting it tentatively in her mouth. "Yum, that's really good, Sra Ana. But you know you don't have to keep bringing me food," she said around a mouthful.

"Yeah, or at least bring enough for everyone," Gabi said pointedly.

Sra Ana gave a little sniff. "This might be the only grand-baby I get. Let me spoil you. Gabriella has been a terrible disappointment to me. I am getting old now and feared I would not hold another baby in these frail arms again." She stooped her back.

Gabi's brows shot skyward. "You know I'm right here, right, Mae?" Deb choked back a laugh, innocently continuing to eat. "I was also there when you helped Papai bring the hay in last week."

Sra Ana waved her daughter's protests aside. "At my age, my memory isn't as good as it used to be." She gave Deb's shoulder a little pat. "Eat up, dear. I will come back later for the dish."

"That's if you remember, Mae," Gabi retorted, snagging another piece from the bowl.

Sra Ana held her hand to her heart, the very picture of a long-suffering parent. "You see how she treats her very own mother?" she moaned. She looked at Deb, her eyes twinkling as she gave a little wink. "If you like, Gabriella, maybe I have some left in the kitchen."

Gabi sprung toward the door. "Why didn't you say so? Enjoy, Deb!" Without a backward glance, she disappeared toward the house.

"Thanks, Sra Ana. For everything," Deb said.

Sra Ana gave her shoulder another gentle squeeze. "You are family. It doesn't always have to be blood to make it so. I will be back later."

Some of the dark cloud that had drifted over Deb lifted a little, not enough for the sun to pierce it yet and light her way, but sometimes all you need is a beginning.

CHAPTER 6

The coolness of the gel was enough to make Deb suck her stomach in. The technician gave her a sympathetic apology. So far, that was the best way to sum it all up. Apologetic. Frankie and Gabi had been sincerely apologetic that they would be away for the appointment. Deb hadn't even bothered to ask Megan, given her surly attitude with the whole Mitch thing, which was pointless since there wasn't even a Mitch thing as far as Deb was concerned. The receptionist had asked if the father was running late and had been embarrassingly apologetic when Deb had muttered that the father wouldn't be attending. The clinical coldness of the ultrasound room seemed oddly apt for the frigid loneliness that held her fast in its grip, sucking her dry of all joy.

"Do you see that little smudge there? Looks like the baby's side," the technician said encouragingly, worried at her patient's detached manner. "Normally you would get your first ultrasound earlier, but since you are much farther along, not that you can tell, I think we might be able to find out the sex." She wiggled the wand, digging lightly into Deb's slightly rounded belly. "Yes, I can definitely see something. Would you like to know?"

It took a few moments for her words to penetrate the fog that permeated Deb's brain. "I guess," she replied dully.

The technician tilted the monitor to enable Deb to have a better view before taking her ice-cold hand in her own. "Honey, can you see the screen clearly?"

Deb raised her gaze. "Yes."

"Well let me introduce you to your daughter."

A tear trickled down Deb's cheek. "A daughter?" she whispered in awe. Her whole body suffused with wonderment which, for the time being, melted some of the icy numbness away.

The hint of a button nose rose out of the fuzzy grey background, the little eyelids still firmly closed. Deb reverently traced the tiny rosebud mouth, a tiny fist held to it. *My daughter.* Even the thought was enough to fill her with an all-encompassing love that lay siege to the cold fear that had a stranglehold on her heart.

"Hi, Deb. Gabi just wanted me to drop this invoice off for her," Mitch said, breaking through her rapture.

Protectively covering the picture with her hand, she looked up from her perch on the bunkhouse stairs. "You can leave it with me. I'll make sure it gets to Gabi's desk."

Mitch took in the quiet. "Where is everyone?"

"Frankie and Gabi are away together again, like usual. And Megan is off doing something—probably anything that doesn't involve me." She was surprised at the bitterness in her voice.

Mitch took his hat off and turned it slowly in his hands. Apparently coming to some sort of decision, he sunk down beside her on the steps. "Are you okay, Deb?"

Deb's face scrunched up in denial. "Why wouldn't I be, Mitch?" And then it was as if the dam wall gave way within her, the words spilling forth. "I'm knocked up, and the father doesn't want anything to do with me or the baby. I know I'm lucky to have the girls, but they're never here, and I know that's unfair, but I need them. Megan isn't talking to me. Well that's not true. When she does talk to me, it's to have a go at me about you. The Cabrera's are awesome, but I feel like I don't deserve it. This isn't how I thought my life would be, living on someone else's ranch as a single soon-to-be mom". A heaving, red-faced, snotty cry broke free from Deb. "I'm surrounded by people, and I am all alone. What if I can't do this? What if I'm no good as a mom?" she wailed.

Mitch pulled her close as the sobs racked her body. "I know it doesn't feel like it right now, but everything is going to be all right."

"You don't know that." Deb sobbed.

"I do know that. You aren't alone. Your friends care about you a lot, and you're going to be a great mom. You are one of the most capable people I know. Heck, I knew that when I asked you to marry me in kindergarten."

Deb gave a watery little smile. "At this rate, I'm going to have to hold you to that proposal."

Mitch gently lifted Deb's chin and stared intently into her eyes. "There would be worse things than being married to you."

Flustered by the look in his eye, Deb's head pounded and swam at the possibility it promised. "Had an ultrasound today," she blurted.

"Is the baby healthy?" Concern made deep furrows appear in his tanned face.

"Yes." She took the ultrasound photo from beneath her hand, gently tracing her baby's face. "Would you like to see?"

"I would be honored." Mitch took the photo from her hand, holding it as if it were the most precious object he had ever been entrusted with. He let out a whistle. "That's one cute anklebiter."

"It's a girl," she said softly.

"Really?" He looked at her excitedly. "A pretty little girl, just like her mommy."

Deb blushed. "I hope she ends up better looking and definitely smarter than me."

Mitch looked at her, his face serious. "I wouldn't change a thing about you." Suddenly, his expression lightened. "This calls for a bloody celebration, and I reckon I know exactly what we should do."

Deb bit her lip, feigning concern. "I'm almost too scared to ask."

"Come on, woman. Get in my car and prepare to be dazzled by my ingenious plan."

She laughed, suddenly feeling light again. These days, it felt like she ran the full gambit of emotions—and that was just before breakfast. "You've got me curious now," she said, rising. "Lead the way".

Mitch looked in danger of bursting with pride at his own cleverness as they pulled up in front of the big white letters emblazoned across the blue background. Deb burst out laughing. "I give up, I'm confused. Why are we at Walmart?"

Mitch gave her a wounded look. "Because, my dear baby-girl-Mommy-to-be, I figure you haven't had a chance to get stuff for the little angel yet. So, to help celebrate your exciting news, my gift to you is that we are going shopping for everything she needs."

Deb was momentarily robbed of the power of speech. How could she explain she had been too scared to buy things for her little girl? That to do so would have been to admit to herself that this was actually going to happen, that she was going to have a baby? Shame rose up in her, despair—her ever constant companion these days—hard on its heels. She hung her head.

"Did I do something wrong?" Mitch sounded panicked. "Please don't cry, Deb. We can leave if you want."

She took a deep breath, her eyes filled with indecisiveness, before gathering herself. "Mitch, you haven't done anything wrong. I just wasn't ready to do it before today." Deb was surprised at the truth ringing through her words, strength starting to flow through her limbs again. "I think I would like very much to go shopping for baby stuff with you."

Mitch looked as if he didn't quite believe her. Or maybe it was just that he wasn't sure what emotion would spill from her next. He gave her hand a squeeze. "Let's bloody do this then."

As they walked across the parking lot, Mitch continued to cast side glances at her. "Okay, what is it?" asked Deb.

Mitch looked unrepentant at being caught. "I was going through names in my head and seeing if they would fit the little tacker."

"I have no baby stuff and I haven't even started thinking of names. I'm the worst mom in the world, aren't I?" Tears threatened again.

Mitch's look of terror returned. "No, no. I'm sure you'll have it all sorted before she makes an arrival. You can borrow one of my names if you like."

Deb blinked her tears away. "What have you got?"

"Lily? No that doesn't seem right. Bess?" Deb shook her head sharply. "You're right. Grace? Anyway, you have plenty of time to pick one. But for now, I reckon we have much more pressing matters to attend to."

Confused, she began to panic as she considered all the things she might have forgotten. Mitch gave her a teasing smile. "Motorized, or push?"

"What?"

"Would madam like a trolley that she pushes or a motor-ized one?"

"I don't think I have ever driven a trolley before," she declared, marveling at the ingenuity to take away all physical effort in shopping.

"You only live once. Decision made," Mitch said, walking beside one. "Your chariot awaits, your majesty."

And thus began one of the most surreal shopping experiences Deb had ever partaken in. Mitch was the perfect gentleman—funny, considerate and attentive. Deb found herself wondering if he was like this with all his girlfriends before shaking the thought clear from her mind. It didn't matter what he was like with his girlfriends. They were friends, and she was pregnant with another man's baby. Mitch stopped his banter when he noticed she had fallen behind. "You coming, Mommy?"

"Sure am, Mitch," she said, accelerating forward.

"Good, 'cause I reckon I just saw a lady walking a bloody big-arsed lizard on a leash."

"Get out! Where the heck is she?" she said, face glowing with excitement.

"I kid you not. In the baby carrier aisle which, incidentally, is where we need to head next if my list is correct." He scootered off, his trolley loaded high with purchases.

Deb gave a happy little smile as she shrugged. *When in Rome...*

CHAPTER 7

The stacks of boxes were uniform in that they all retained a precarious lean to the side. So much as a hint of a breeze would likely be enough to send their precious contents tumbling to the ground. Amidst this precarious environment, Deb sat, legs crossed as she basked in the warm glow of—dare she say it—happiness. She rubbed her belly as she contemplated the shift in her emotional well-being, checking carefully for the cold ball of fear. Unable to locate any traces of it, she breathed in, luxuriating in the almost-forgotten feeling.

The slam of a kitchen cupboard shook her out of her Zen-like state. *It was good while it lasted,* she mused as she pushed herself up off the floor. Knocking her knee as she crossed the room, she gave the offending box a threatening glare. She really needed to look at assembling the glider chair or at least move it out of the way, but that was tomorrow's problem. Through the open doorway of Frankie's old room, she eyeballed Megan as she huffed about the kitchen, tension radiating from the tight set of her shoulders. *This was going to be fun.*

"Hi, Megan. Is there anything in particular you are

looking for, or are you just enjoying taking your displeasure out on the innocent cabinetry?" she asked drily.

"Not all of us get our meals delivered you know," Megan acidly replied, continuing to forage through the pantry. "Or just skip off for most of the day and leave others to do all the work for that matter."

A twinge of guilt vibrated through Deb. "I'm sorry about that. I thought I'd told you about my ultrasound today."

"You said you would be done by lunchtime."

"I was. I came back, and you were nowhere to be found. Then Mitch took me to get some baby stuff." Deb mentally rolled her eyes. *Like that was going to make this better.*

"Oh, so you just assumed I didn't need any help? What, not even a quick call to see if I was okay? For your information, I was at the feed store picking up some more wormers for the horses, then I had to go to the saddlery to get the rugs they mended, and then I went to the hardware and got some fencing wire because we're out and the new mares went through a fence last night. Oh, and a quick trip to get more first aid supplies from the vet." During her tirade, Megan's voice progressively got louder and higher pitched. "So, while you're off on shopping trips with lover boy, I'm keeping this stud going, and I'm getting bloody sick of it."

"Look, I'm sorry, but don't you think that's a little unfair? It was one shopping trip, and Mitch is just a friend."

"Oh, come on. He's following you around like a lovesick puppy. It makes me want to puke." Megan said hotly, slamming her hands down on the kitchen counter in frustration. "You know what?" She spun around angrily. "I wish I had never bloody come here. Everyone has someone else. Frankie has everyone and everything. She doesn't have time for me. You have Mitch and this baby. But what about me? I'm just good enough to keep everything going and sometimes I get thrown a few crumbs."

Deb stood frozen, taken aback by the unexpected

outburst from her friend. Guilt wormed its way deeper into her heart. What kind of a friend was she to not know this was how Megan was feeling? She took a tentative step forward.

"Megan, I had no idea. I'm so sorry you feel this way. I swear I'll try harder around here." Remorse etched a hard groove in her forehead. "I know I've been caught up in this pregnancy thing, but that's no excuse to not know how you've been feeling."

Megan gave a frustrated sniffle. "It's not all your fault. I mean, I get you have a lot going on. It's just that I really like Mitch and, just this once, I wanted it to be me, you know?"

"He's just a friend. But you're one of my best friends and I love you, even if you've been a bit of a cow lately."

Megan's lips quirked. "I probably deserve that. I might have been a bit difficult to be around lately."

Deb snorted. "A bit? I reckon that's the understatement of the year!"

"Fine. I'm sorry, too. I can't promise I won't get jealous with Mitch giving you attention, but I'll try not to revert to full cow mode."

"I meant what I said. You're one of my best friends. I've missed you, and with this little one coming"—Deb rubbed her belly gently, a soft smile on her lips—"I really need you."

Megan gave another sniff, drained of her anger. "Aww, come here." She pulled her into a rough hug, careful not to squeeze too hard. "So everything is okay with the baby?" she asked as she released Deb.

"I'm having a little barrel racer. It's a girl!" she announced proudly.

Megan pulled her into another quick hug. "I'm going to be an auntie to a little girl. Heaven help me."

"Well this little girl wants Tim Tams. Do you think I can find any over here?" Deb said, changing the subject.

"I'm sure if anyone can, it'll be you," Megan said, laughing.

〜

"You're where?" exclaimed Deb.

"The hospital. Look, they're bloody trying to make out it's more than it is. I'm slightly concussed and have some stitches, not completely cactus. It's like they've never seen a bloke that's copped one from a mule before," Mitch said through the phone.

Deb choked on her laughter. "Sorry, what did you say? A mule?"

"Yes, a mule." He sighed in exasperation. "Look, I can tell you the full story when you come and pick me up. You will come and get me, right?"

"Well, I was going to wash my hair tonight, but now I need to get the story about this mule. Guess I'd better come sort you out."

"Gee, thanks. See ya soon."

Megan looked up curiously, obviously intrigued by the one-sided conversation she had overheard. "Do I even want to know?"

"Yeah, nah. I'll give you all the details once I extract them from Mitch. From what I can gather, he's got a concussion, so I reckon it might be best if I bring him back here and he can sleep on the couch tonight."

"Nurse Deb to the rescue," Megan teased. "I'll make up the couch for him while you're out."

"Thanks." Deb grabbed her keys off the counter. "Oh, and Megan?"

"Yeah?"

"I know the exact number of Tim Tams I have left, too. Don't even think about it."

"Frank is the mule?" Megan asked.

Mitch gingerly perched on the couch to pull his boots off, the large purplish contusion at his temple in stark contrast against the pale flesh. Deb thought he looked kind of cute sitting there all banged up and feeling sorry for himself. She hadn't noticed the little pale band of skin just below his hairline where his tan stopped before. A side effect of working out in the sun wearing a hat.

"No, Frank was the pig. Also known as Frank the Tank to his friends," he sourly replied.

"I thought you said a mule kicked you," Deb said.

"A mule did," he muttered.

"What was the mule called, then?"

Mitch mumbled something incoherently.

Deb leaned forward. "I didn't quite catch that."

Mitch leaned back in the couch and crossed his arms over his chest, a what could only be described as an ornery expression fixed on his face. Amused, Deb was rather unkindly starting to see a resemblance to the mule in the story.

"Princess Gertrude Merrytoes," he ground out.

Megan's brow wrinkled. "I'm confused. What does Frank have to do with you getting kicked?"

Mitch stubbornly thrust his jaw out. "Earlier today, I was hungry. So I pulled into a diner. I didn't check the bloody booth before I sat and ended up sitting in some spilt grub—eggs and bacon to be precise. Anyway, I cleaned myself up and got on with my day."

"Get to the good part," Deb instructed, impatiently shooing him along with her hand.

"So, I'm trimming Princess Gertrude Merrytoes's hooves, and she's best friends with bloody Frank the Tank. I didn't really think too much about him sniffing around, but he must have smelled his relative on my backside. Next minute, Frank has a mouthful of my bloody butt. I start screaming blue murder, which must have pissed Princess Gertrude

Merrytoes off. She lets off an almighty wallop and kicks me in the head."

Deb gave a little cough, Mitch looked at her suspiciously. "So, these stitches you mentioned earlier … are where, exactly?"

Mitch looked at her, his face pinched as color suffused it. "My backside. The stitches are on my bloody backside."

The girls exploded into peals of laughter as he sourly watched them succumb to their hysterics.

Long after Megan had excused herself to go to bed, Deb lounged in the overstuffed armchair opposite Mitch. A companionable exhaustion pleasantly filled her body as they both watched the television together. Maybe this is what it would be like to have a man to settle down with? She could imagine, after a long day of both working, coming home and sitting together after putting the baby to bed. No need for conversation to fill in the silence. Just this wonderful feeling of being perfectly in sync. A sharp jab caught her off guard, causing her to exclaim in consternation.

Mitch looked at her in alarm. "Are you all right?"

Deb pressed her hands to her stomach in wonder. "I think she might have just kicked me." She gave another little jump as the jab came again. "She just did it again!"

Mitch looked at her in amazement. "Strewth, is she meant to be kicking already?"

She smiled gently, her face soft as she cradled her belly. "Yep."

Jaw slack, Mitch fixed his gaze on her. "What does it feel like?"

Deb turned her attention inward focusing on every twitch she felt. "Like butterflies are fluttering about in my belly. It's hard to describe, but it feels magical. Would you like to feel it?"

"Is it okay? I mean, I don't want to hurt the little blighter."

Deb smiled affectionately at the banged-up farrier, stitches in places he'd rather they weren't, concussion and all. And he was worried he would hurt her baby. "Come here and give me your hand."

Hesitantly, he complied. She gently held his hand to her stomach. After a few moments, Mitch began to pull away. "Maybe that's all she feels like doing for tonight."

"Shh," she admonished, patiently waiting for her daughter to make a move. A sharp jab pushed against the hand in protest. "There," she said in satisfaction, smiling up at Mitch. "Did you feel that?"

A look of wonderment fanned across his face before he broke into a beaming smile. "I sure did."

Deb proudly cradled her belly. "She's a strong little thing, isn't she?"

Mitch, his eyes lingering on her face, gave a lopsided smile. "Just like her beautiful mommy."

Deb's heart did a funny little flip-flop as his blue eyes looked deeply into hers, his warm hand still pressing against her rounded stomach. Feeling flustered, she stood suddenly, her large belly hitting Mitch in the face and knocking him off balance. He toppled backwards and let out a yelp of pain as his backside made contact with the floor.

"Bloody heck. I'm sorry, Mitch," she apologized as she helped him to his feet. It was made all the more comical by her belly once again getting in the way, this time of being able to bend over fully.

"As long as you bloody promise not to make any sudden moves where my butt is concerned, I'll forgive you," he said painfully, gently settling himself onto the couch.

"I think that's my cue to say goodnight," Deb said.

"I didn't mean you had to go to bed."

"It's past my bedtime anyway, and these days, this little princess"—she looked down fondly at her belly—"wakes me up, like, a million times having to go to the bathroom." Deb blushed sheepishly, suddenly conscious she might have over-shared a little too much personal information.

Mitch grinned at her. "She's helping you get your steps in for the day."

Deb snorted. "Mate, I get more than enough just with moving all of the horses around before I even do anything else around the ranch. And on that note, I'll say goodnight."

"Goodnight, Deb. I hope the little princess lets you get some sleep," Mitch said.

As Deb closed the door, she got a final glimpse of Mitch settling himself onto the couch. A feeling of contentment stole over her, her baby clearly sharing the sentiment by kicking again. "I like him being here, too," she whispered. "But it's only for tonight."

CHAPTER 8

*P*ink bunting hung festively from the live oak tree. Soft blankets scattered with pastel-hued cushions were spread beneath. Hay bales had been arranged with timber tops to form low grazing tables laden with pink-themed treats. Even the centerpiece pavlova had been decorated with strawberries, the raspberry coulee tinting the whipped cream pink. Frankie and Sra Ana fluttered about making sure all the finishing touches were perfect.

Deb momentarily experienced a disorientating sensation of standing trapped on the outside looking in on the scene before her. Trying to shake the ominous sense of not belonging, she protectively cradled her belly. But it did nothing to ease the chill of estrangement.

Frankie bustled over, a broad grin on her face. "What do you think?" She gestured to her handiwork.

"I think that this little girl had better like pink." Deb absently rubbed her lower back as she looked around. A dull ache had settled there overnight. She looked forward to curling up in bed with a hot wheat bag once the baby shower was finished.

Her friend looked to be on the verge of saying something,

a ping interrupting the thought. "Dang, I forgot the cake server. Deb are you able to grab the spare one from the bunkhouse?"

"Sure thing. I can get us one, but I think I have an easier idea than walking all the way over there," Deb replied, waddling toward Sra Ana. "Sra Ana, we need a cake server. Can we borrow one from the house?"

If Deb didn't know better, she would have thought Sra Ana was up to something. She swallowed several times, her eyes guiltily darting about before settling briefly on Frankie as if having some sort of silent communication. "I don't have one," she said with aplomb.

"Didn't you have one last week when you made the chocolate cake?" Deb said, eyebrows raised suspiciously.

"It broke. Yes, that's what happened. It broke and I threw it away." Relieved at having come up with a plausible reason, a smile broke out on her face, easing the nervous tension of earlier.

Deb narrowed her eyes suspiciously. "Okay," she said slowly. "Looks like I'll head to the bunkhouse and get the one from there then." As she waddled her way over, she glanced down at her belly. "I love them all dearly, but sometimes they sure as heck are bloody strange."

"That's right send the pregnant whale lady up the flight of stairs with some lame excuse why don't you?" Deb muttered under her breath as she huffed and puffed her way up to the bunkhouse. At the top of the stairs, she paused, attempting to regain her breath, conscious now that her lungs were beginning to run out of room.

"Geeze, you're starting to squish mommy's innards a bit there, baby girl." She made her way through the door and stopped dead in her tracks. "What are you doing here?" she asked Mitch, her voice raised in surprised.

"I know the baby shower is a bit of a ladies only event, but I wanted to give you something special today as well," Mitch said, striding forward to take her hand in his.

Deb looked at him nervously, a thrumming in her chest as confusion pummeled her heart. "You've done enough with all the stuff you got me when you took me shopping."

"That was just stuff. This is something special." He gave a gentle tug on her hand to set her feet in motion and led her to the nursery. Deb stopped, dumbfounded. Her eyes went wide as they settled on the cradle that took pride of place in the room. Creamy timber sides had been lovingly hand carved with horse motifs. Deb ran her hand reverently over the wood, marveling at the smooth warm texture. A bed fit for her little cowgirl princess.

"I'm speechless," she said simply, unable to take her eyes off the heartfelt masterpiece.

"This from the girl Mrs Humprey said in first grade could talk underwater with a mouthful of marbles," Mitch teased. "So, you like it then?"

"Like it? That's kinda like saying I like my coffee. And we all know how much I love that." She laughed as her baby girl made her presence known. "Well, you get her vote. But seriously, it's beautiful. Nope that's not right either." Mitch looked wounded. "It's glorious. Thank you." She said, once again lost in its beauty.

"I started making this the day you told me you were pregnant." He looked at her earnestly. "Deb, it's just … ah, bloody heck." He raked his hands through his hair. "You're special, and that little tacker in your belly, she's as special as her mom to me."

Deb gently traced the carved outline of a prancing unicorn, each stroke painstakingly intricate, her heart thumping. Mitch cleared his throat. "Cat got your tongue?

Mrs Humprey will be turning in her grave," he said, trying to lighten the mood.

Deb finally raised her eyes to meet his hopeful ones. She considered her words carefully. "You've been a good friend for most of my life. Well, except for those lost years when you ran off and tried the whole city thing." She cradled her belly gently. "You're special to me, too. Well, us." She was afraid the vulnerability she felt showed in her eyes as he stepped closer. "I'm not very good at this. I haven't really made the best life choices where men are concerned. More of a love 'em and leave 'em type."

Mitch was now so close she could feel his breath intimately warming the flesh on her forehead. "I think you're doing just fine. But we have all the time in the world to figure out how to do this." He softly kissed the top of her head. A flash of disappointment flared, surprising Deb when she realized that was the only move he was going to make. "Now, I promised both Sra Ana and Frankie I wouldn't take you away from your baby shower for too long. Between you and me, I'm a bit scared of the new and improved married Frankie, but don't ever tell her that."

Deb chuckled. "Our little Frankie is all grown up. She had to be, too, with a man like Luciano. She was difficult before, but she's impossible now. It's awesome."

Mitch offered his arm. "Well then, my ladies, both born and otherwise, will you allow me to escort you back to your party?"

She laughed brightly. "Lead the way, sir."

～

"Psst, what have you written down for this one?" Megan whispered.

"Pea, couscous, Vegemite, and asparagus." Deb rubbed her aching back, the cramping getting worse. As far as she was concerned, it was dang inconvenient timing to be having Braxton Hicks. Taking another spoonful from the unlabeled jar, she swirled the baby food around her mouth, attempting to identify the ingredients. "There could be a hint of fetta in there as well."

"Really? I had carrot and bacon mush," whispered Gabi, sidling up. "How on earth are all of these babies so chubby if they're eating this slop?"

"I didn't even know you could get so many different flavors. I was shocked when I went to buy these." Frankie said, joining the conversation. "Now, write down your answers so we can move on to 'guess the baby'."

Megan rolled her eyes. "You just like thinking about what a Luciano baby will look like."

A sharp pain hit Deb, squeezing the breath from her lungs. She let out a low moan. Frankie quickly grabbed her arm. "Deb, what's wrong? Megan, get a chair for her. Gabi, I think we need your mom here pronto."

The bands of pain relaxed their grip on Deb, the ability to once again draw oxygen and process thought returned. She looked up into her friends' concerned faces as Sra Ana bustled over. "It's fine. Just some Braxton Hicks. The books said they can make you feel like it's the real thing for newbies. Don't stress, it's way too early for anything more."

Sra Ana's expression was grave. "How long have you been having these?"

"Well, it just felt like period cramps last night. My back got worse a few hours ago. The pain just then was something new."

The older Brazilian woman's face pinched with worry. "Stay sitting here. I will get you some water. Gabi, go get something for her to put her feet up on." She pursed her lips. "I think it is best that at least one of us stays with you at all times until these pains stop."

Deb smiled fondly at her fussing. "Thanks, Sra Ana, but I'm built tough. This is just the warmup for the main event."

Sra Ana's eyes remained troubled. Despite the smile she gave for the young woman's benefit. "I pray you are right."

~

The pain ratcheted through Deb's body, all thought fleeing before it. She drew in a shuddering breath. "I don't think I can do this. It's too early."

Frankie grasped her hand. "You are the most determined, strongest person I know." She glanced at the other women in the room guiltily. "Present company excluded, obviously. Girl, you've got this."

Another wave of pain slammed into Deb hard. "Help me, please someone help me." She whimpered.

Megan went pale in the face. "The midwife said it's too late for an epidural, but there's gotta be something else they can give her?"

Sra Ana rubbed the laboring girl's back. "Deb, you need to look at me." Deb raised her bloodshot eyes, locking onto the older woman's as if a lifeline from her agony. "Sweetheart, ride each wave as it comes. Breathe. Soon you will hold your baby girl in your arms." She smiled over at her daughter sweetly. "And then you will have a lifetime of trouble and worry."

"Hey, I'm standing right here," Gabi protested. "Seriously, Deb, you can do this." She huddled with Megan. "I'm scared."

Megan put an arm around her. "Me too," she whispered.

Sra Ana looked sympathetically at the pair of girls. "How about you take a break and go see if the menfolk are okay?" she suggested.

Neither girl had to be asked twice and, with an apologetic hurried look at their laboring friend, fled the room.

Deb groaned as another contraction hit. She gripped Frankie's hand tightly. "Promise me the baby will be okay."

"I promise I won't let anything happen to you or the baby," Frankie swore, looking over Deb's head worriedly to the midwife and Sra Ana.

With each contraction, pain dominated Deb's entire being. The torment of labor became a prison for her mind. In those moments, those seconds that stretched her mind and body to breaking point, there was nothing else. When the pain passed, it was only for a minute or so. She breathed with closed eyes, unable to leave her shattered consciousness.

The night was long and unending, but finally, a relieved Frankie looked down into her friend's exhausted face. Pure joy shone through her tears. "She's beautiful, Deb. You did so good."

Deb looked down at the blanket-covered bundle, a tiny scrunched up face peeking out. She could feel her daughter's warmth, sticky against her skin. Love, so primal in its potency it scared her with its strength, flowed through her. "My daughter. Frankie, this is my daughter."

Sra Ana stroked the new mother's head gently. "A new generation for our extended family. Both Eduardo and I are so very proud."

"Have you decided what you are going to call her?" Frankie asked, instantly besotted.

"Grace. Her name is Grace."

Frankie sniffled. "I don't think I can handle how beautiful she is, Deb."

Grace began to give little grunting noises as she struggled with each breath. The midwives bustled in, placing a tiny mask over the baby's face. "We need to take her to NICU. But don't worry, Mama. We will take good care of her." One swiftly wrapped Grace more securely in the blanket before placing her in a portable incubator and wheeling her from the room. The other handed a care package to Sra Ana. "The showers are through there. Once she has showered and changed, her room will be ready." The midwife left, giving the women privacy.

"Do you need a hand getting up?" Frankie hesitantly said, unsure how best to aid her friend.

"I think I'll be okay," Deb said tiredly, rolling onto her side and lowering her feet to the floor. A sharp pain in her nether regions reminded her of exactly what she had just been through.

"Do you want one of us to help with the shower or—" Frankie fluttered about, uncertain.

Sra Ana gently took Deb by the arm and slowly escorted her to the shower room, glancing at a worried Frankie as she passed. "I have placed everything you need here." She gestured to the little shelf as she lowered Deb onto the plastic shower chair. "The button is here if you need help, but both Frankie and I will be waiting outside the door. Call us if you need anything." She gave the exhausted mother one last look and closed the door.

The adrenaline left Deb's body in great waves, leaving her shattered by the emotions rocking her, unable to process what she had experienced. As the warm water washed the grime of birth away from her body, she sobbed quietly, her body quivering.

Audible beeping accompanied the flickering lines that danced across the monitor's screen, eerily reflected on the new mother's face as she gazed intently into the humidicrib. Mitch stood quietly, hesitant to interrupt Deb's vigil of her daughter. It was confronting to see such a tiny, fragile body hooked up to tubes.

His mind flashed back to the torturous hours of waiting for her safe delivery. Waiting outside with the other men, he hadn't known what to expect when he would finally be able to see her. The urgency that had wailed through him screamed out that he should be in there with her easing her pain. Instead, he had stood outside helpless in the face of her agony, the night dragging on until, in the wee hours of the morning, silence. His ears strained for a hint of noise. And there it was, the most glorious sound. A thin baby's wail. A sound that he wasn't even aware was the moment the tiny infant stole his heart as surely as its mother had.

Now he stood on the threshold of the room, uncertain if Deb knew how he felt or if he should dare hope that she returned his feelings.

"She's beautiful, isn't she?" she asked softly, her voice exhausted.

"She's a cracker." He came closer, looking at the precious little soul. "Hello, Grace. Welcome to the outside. Have they told you how long she needs to stay here before you can take her home?"

"They said she needs to do a lot of things on her own before they will even start talking about a home date." Her breath came out in a shaky quiver, her fingers trembling as she gently touched the humidicrib, the distance between her and her daughter insurmountable. "I love her so much. But this"—she put her forehead against the smooth plastic—"I don't know how to do this."

"You're already doing what you're meant to be doing," he said. "You're loving her and worrying over her. That's what a mom does."

Deb's shoulders began to shake. Mitch took her in his

arms, trying to put all his love and comfort into the embrace while he battled internally with a sense of helplessness. How could he ever make her see the sense of wonder he felt at her strength, to have created this child? But there was one thing he did know—he would do anything for this woman and her baby.

CHAPTER 9

Frankie bounced as she flopped down in the hospital chair. "She's looking really good."

Deb looked down at her sleeping daughter, the rasping of her breathing noisy in the otherwise quiet room. "They said the PIC line should be removed by the end of the week, and she'll be doing everything by herself. Then it's just a matter of getting her weight up to where it should be."

Her friend smiled, a clucky expression on her face. "That's awesome. Seriously, she's so cute I could eat her up."

Deb reached for the machine positioned on the table beside her. "Do you mind?" she asked, gesturing to it. "But I need to express."

Frankie looked a little flustered. "Um, yeah, no. I mean, the girl has to eat after all." She shook her head with a self-deprecating smile. "Sorry, I'm being silly. Does it hurt?"

"Only when it's been a while between doing it, like if I have a sleep or something. It did feel strange the first time they stuck it on me. All I could think about was when I used to work at the dairy." Deb felt doubt swirl around her, pulling her in. Everything she had read said breastfeeding was important for the health of the baby and to help them bond. Failure slammed hard into her. She couldn't even take care of the fundamental basics for her daughter.

Deb adjusted her top to cover most of the cup on her breast, fiddling with the fabric to get it to sit right. The machine made a whirring noise. "Um, Deb. You okay?" Frankie queried at her friend's continued silence.

She blinked as if returning from wherever her mind had wandered, startled to find herself once again in a sterile hospital room. "Yeah, fine."

Deb thought Frankie didn't seem overly convinced by her reply, but she was saved from having to say anything more by Mitch's arrival.

"Hello, Mitch," Frankie said, returning his greeting. Deciding to leave the two of them alone with the slumbering baby, she stood. "Well, I had better get a wiggle on. It's Luc's turn to cook. He said it's a surprise, which I find slightly concerning." Mitch and Deb laughed, and once again, Frankie gave her that indiscernible look. "Gabi and I will be back in a week and I'll come and see you then. But I'll call you while we're gone anyway." She smiled teasingly up at Mitch. "I'm sure this big, strapping bloke here will keep you company while I'm gone."

Mitch gave Deb's leg a little pat where it lay on the bed. "You can count on it, Frankie," he replied solemnly before a mischievous twinkle entered his eye. "That's if Sra Ana doesn't hog her and the baby."

Frankie laughed. "That's true. She is rather besotted with Grace, but that's 'cause Gabi and Carlos won't step up to the plate and give her any grandbabies of her own." She gave Deb a hug. "Look after yourself while I'm gone, okay?" She paused to give Deb one last look before leaving the room.

Mitch parked himself in the chair Frankie had recently vacated, averting his eyes when Deb switched the expressing cup to the other breast. Grace gave a little hiccupping gurgle as she awoke. "So, how has the little princess cowgirl been today?" he crooned to the bub. Deb reached for the call button. "Sleeping a lot and still hard work to get a burp out of. But other than that, she's a good baby. Well, as far as I can tell."

A nurse bustled in. "All done?" She gestured to the bottle Deb was securing a lid on.

"I'm staying abreast of it, if that's what you mean," Deb responded. The nurse remained calmly professional, not allowing a hint of a smile to appear. "I'm sorry for the joke. I've made a bit of a boob of myself, haven't I?"

Mitch snorted. "I think you need to nip that in the bud, right now. It's seems like you have been milking it a bit, going by your nurse's reaction."

The stony-faced nurse secured a teat to the bottle. "Would you like to feed her this time, Dad?"

"Oh, I'm not the dad."

"Yeah, he's not the—"

Both Mitch and Deb spoke at the same time, their words stumbling over each other.

The nurse finally smiled, albeit a little awkwardly. "I'm sorry. I just assumed, since you're here all the time." She offered the bottle to Deb.

Deb looked down at the proffered bottle and then to Mitch, her eyes questioning. "Would you like to feed her, Mitch?"

His mouth dropped open, before shutting with a clink and tears welled in his eyes. For a moment, Deb was worried he might have bitten his tongue. "I would be honored," he said sincerely. The nurse picked Grace up from her crib and, as she prepared to hand her to Mitch, he threw his hands up in protest. "Easy there, give a bloke some warning. How do I do it?"

The nurse looked at him, confused. "Do what?"

Deb burst out laughing, taking pity on him. "He means how does he hold the baby."

"Don't drop it. Think you can remember that? Now, sit," the nurse commanded sternly, her tone belied by the gentleness that she deposited the baby into the worried man's arms.

Mitch sat stiffly upright, his chest barely rising and falling as if worried the babe would break. "Here." The nurse said gruffly, thrusting the bottle at his face. Mitch raised his hand in self-defense and found himself suddenly in the possession of it. "She needs to drink all of it, and then give her a burp. You got all of that?"

"Yes, ma'am."

"Good." And without another word, the nurse sailed from the room.

Deb rather admired her handling of the situation, even if she did feel a teeny bit contrite for enjoying it quite so much. Mitch smiled ruefully, never taking his eyes off Grace blissfully suckling the bottle. "Bloody heck. Is she always such a barrel of laughs?"

"Pretty much."

A companionable silence stretched, filled only with little slurps and gurgles. "How are you doing, Mommy? And I mean a real answer. Not fine or something like that."

The world around her retracted as she attempted to articulate her feelings, her heart pounding in her throat as the anxiety threatened to overwhelm her. "I have never loved something as much as I love her. But I'm terrified I'm going to stuff up, that I'm not good enough for her. That she deserves more. Sometimes I feel a black cloud hover over me, and I'm scared the darkness will hurt her."

Mitch watched her as she spoke, his expression non-judgmental as he digested her words. "No one will love her as much as you do. You have a mother's love."

"But what if that isn't enough?"

"That love will move mountains. If it doesn't, I will help you move them for her."

Deb looked away, unable to handle the tenderness his eyes emitted. She wasn't worthy of it. "Mitch, we aren't your problem."

Grace began to fuss with the bottle, so Mitch gently put her over his shoulder and began to pat her on the back. "Come on you little tacker, give Mitch a burp," he crooned. "I want you to be my problem, Deb."

A tsunami of emotions buffeted her like she was a leaf in a storm, the fear laying siege to the longing for what he offered her and winning. Her eyes clouded over. "Everything is just so hard right now."

"But it doesn't have to be. We can make it easy as pie if we want to."

"What happens if all we're meant to be is friends? I don't want to risk our friendship by trying to make it more than it should be."

Grace gave a resounding burp. "Good girl," Mitch said as he stood. He gave Grace a kiss on her button nose. "Be good for your mommy," he said as he handed her to Deb. "I think you're worth it. There's nothing you could ever do that would make me turn my back on you." As he straightened, he paused, his eyes level with hers, a promise shining forth. He kissed her softly, his lips a faint whisper on her own. "Goodnight, Deb. I'll see you tomorrow."

Deb watched him leave, terror and hope warring within her. In her arms, her baby slept peacefully.

CHAPTER 10

"Give me a moment. The instructions said that it should click in," Senhor Eduardo muttered, his voice muffled as he leaned over the baby capsule. Grace cooed as his hair tickled her face.

"Papai, let me have a go," Gabi ordered.

"I know what I am doing, Gabriella," he replied gruffly. "Don't I, bebe?" Grace cooed in agreement. Senhor Eduardo winced as she tugged on his hair.

"I give up. Take all the time you want." Gabi threw her hands in the air in defeat and settled down beside Deb and Sra Ana. "I'm glad I didn't take after him and his stubbornness."

Deb spluttered on the mouthful of water she had just sipped, the drink spraying forth with gusto as she coughed. Sra Ana patted her on the back, looking at her earnest-faced daughter. "Yes, we are indeed lucky."

Gabi nodded happily at her mother's comment. "The girls are waiting for us at the ranch. Frankie flies out tonight to meet up with Luciano. But she is super excited to welcome Grace home."

Deb's forehead wrinkled as she watched Senhor Eduardo

wage battle on the capsule. "Thank you for coming and getting me—us," she corrected herself.

Sra Ana reached an understanding hand to Deb, her eyes kind. "Deb, you and Grace are family. This is what family does. Now, if I had my way, you would be moving into the main house with that precious bebe where I could look after you both."

Gabi rolled her eyes. "Deb doesn't need a mother hen hovering around. Anyway, Deb's home is the bunkhouse with the rest of us. Isn't that right?"

"I am triumphant!" Senhor Eduardo proudly exclaimed. "Ladies, your chariot awaits."

"Finally," Gabi said, giving her father a cheeky look.

"So, it is my fault you have given me no grandbabies to practice on?"

"That's your comeback?" Gabi asked her father.

"I forgive you for treating your mae and poor papai so badly. But Deb is now my favorite." With a mischievous wink in Deb's direction, he opened the truck door and ushered the women in.

It was like looking through the lens of a camera. The scene laid before her was achingly familiar in an annoyingly disorientating way. The evocative aroma of the horses still pungent, the mundane sound of their movements chasing the quiet away. And yet none of it seemed the same as before, no longer the call of safety and home. Her overwhelmingly peculiar reaction to returning to the ranch struck Deb as bizarre. The epiphany hit hard as she trod the well-worn steps to the bunkhouse, the baby capsule heavy on her arm. Her steps were made heavy by the sudden comprehension that it wasn't the ranch that had changed, but her.

When she had first entered the barn over a year ago, she

had been confident in her ability to handle anything life could throw her way. How naïve had she been? Now she doubted everything. It was as if she was a hollow shell, a caricature of the vivacious young woman she had been. Her only saving grace now was her daughter.

She was dimly aware of her friends chattering excitedly around her on the extreme edge of her periphery. It was as if they talked to her from another room. Her feet, unbidden, took her to the threshold of the nursery, the door swinging freely, silent on freshly oiled hinges. She stopped dead in her tracks.

Inside, the late afternoon sun softly shone in, making golden puddles of light on the floor. The Holly Hobbie patterned curtains fluttered in the breeze. The rocking chair she never had quite managed to construct was in the corner, complete with a footrest. The shelf above, a new edition, displayed a pink teddy bear and a patchwork rag doll, against a backdrop of prancing carousal horse wallpaper. The little table beside it held a basket filled with wrapped cookies and dried fruits.

"I read lactation cookies help with milk," offered Megan. "And then I got Frankie to make some for you." She grinned sheepishly. "'Cause I wanted you to actually be able to eat them."

A pink throw rug hung over the backrest of the chair, matching the circular rug in the middle of the room perfectly. Pride of place was taken by the cradle Mitch had so lovingly crafted, now with a matching chest of drawers complete with a change table on top. As Deb ran her hand tentatively over the smooth sanded timber, a ringing sound began in her ears.

"Mitch said the little cowgirl princess needed matching furniture," Gabi offered.

"Do you like it?" asked Frankie, sounding concerned.

A heavy weight settled over Deb at the sight of perfection

her friends had created. She hardly dared breath as if her very presence in the room would somehow tarnish the flawless composition. Abject despair robbed the last flicker of confidence she possessed. Her friends were able to create this for her daughter when she hadn't even been able to assemble the rocking chair. Two fat tears rolled wordlessly down Deb's face as the baby fussed in her arms.

"Deb?"

"I just—I need to get some air." Deb bolted from the room, leaving dumbfounded silence in her wake.

~

The plaintive wail of her baby fussing at the tears splashing down on her broke through Deb's trance. She looked around, bewildered to have found herself outside Delila's stall, the buckskin mare curiously snuffling at her salty face.

A gentle hand touched her arm. "It can be overwhelming, motherhood. May I have a hold?"

Deb looked up at Sra Ana's softly understanding face, taken with how naturally she held Grace. "I don't mean to be ungrateful. The nursery is beautiful. I don't know what's bloody wrong with me." Her eyes beseeched the older woman for an answer. "I feel like I'm going mad." She finished, miserable.

"You have been through a lot since the birth of your daughter, and then the time in hospital. Nothing has been easy for you. Maybe you need to take your time and breathe." Sra Ana swayed peacefully as she rocked the baby.

"That's the thing. I don't know that I can. Sometimes I can't even draw in air. I love Grace so much, but she doesn't deserve a mother that's such a mess."

"Deb, look at me." She raised her downcast eyes to connect with Sra Ana's wise and understanding ones. "What Grace needs is her mother. You are enough. And if you ever feel like you aren't, remember you aren't alone. She is surrounded by strong women who love her, and I would like to think Eduardo and I are her family too. There is also a certain farrier that I have noticed is rather taken with both her and her mother." Fondness twinkled in her eyes.

Deb struggled to form words over the stubbornly lodged lump of misery, her throat painfully constricted. As Sra Ana cooed at the baby, a picture of maternal contentment, her own sense of inadequacy was only further compounded. Balancing the baby in one arm, the older woman wordlessly put an arm around Deb. The sun gently slipped toward the horizon, casting long shadows over the little group. The girl sobbed as she was gently rocked in rhythm with her daughter.

Deb swayed back and forth in the rocking chair, the soothing motion causing her eyes to partially close on the verge of drifting off into an exhausted sleep. Feeling Gracie's weight become limp, she judged that she would soon be able to settle her into her cradle. Her friend's words began to wash over her, soothing in their cadence

"Sampson is due to cover Delila this week, if signs of cycling continue. How long are you going to be away this time?" Megan asked quietly.

"Two weeks for this run," Frankie replied softly. "Gabi will drive the horses to the next rodeo a couple of times while I fly off to see Luciano."

"I've been thinking..." Megan paused for a moment as if searching for the right words. "I can't keep up with the horses in work here. Not long term, not with everything else I have to do. And I don't think Deb will be coming back in any capacity for a while."

Frankie sighed heavily. "I don't want to agree, but you're

right. Deb has to deal with whatever is going on right now and get healthy." How could Frankie say that? How could any of them say that? None of them had kids, they didn't understand what it was like to have a baby. "She needs to focus on Grace. I only have another two months left of hauling for the year, not that that really helps you right now. Leave it with me, and I'll talk to Gabi about getting someone in to take some of the load off you. The problem will be finding the right person."

"Thanks, Frankie. Training has never really been my thing. Deb doesn't mind it, but neither of us are like you."

"And I'm not around enough at the moment to be of much help," Frankie added.

"That's not what I meant. You're out there on the road getting the ranch's name on the map. You're doing your job."

"I know that's not what you meant, but it's how I feel. Like, right now, I need to be here, rather than out there."

Did Frankie really believe she needed to look after her? Did she think that she was that bad a mother that she needed to watch over her? The betrayal Deb felt at Frankie's words left a bitter taste in her mouth. Gently, she rose to her feet and laid Grace down in her cradle. She choked back a sob. Even her friends thought she was a burden—just another thing they needed to try and fit into their perfect lives.

A knock interrupted her line of thought. Outside, she could hear someone padding over to the door.

"Gabi, since when did you start knocking?" Frankie's voice called out, followed by the creak of the door opening.

"Well, hello, darlin'. Did you miss me?" Deb felt her jaw drop open in surprise, she knew that voice anywhere—Tucker Brown.

CHAPTER 11

"*W*ell, did you?"

Deb felt like she had entered a real life movie as entered the room. A single glance showed her Frankie, nostrils flared, shutting her mouth with an audible clink, and Tucker Brown grinning insolently, one hand holding the door frame. Appearing to gather her wits, she swung the door hard as if to make the vision before her disappear. Tucker's hand slammed into the wood as he stopped it, making each of the girls jump in alarm.

He pushed it open forcefully, stepping into the room. "Now, what sort of welcome is that to a new father?"

"Grace was born six weeks ago. Anyway, weren't you the one who didn't want anything to do with her? You have some hide showing up here after how you have treated Deb." Color suffused Frankie's face, her finger jabbing into the air between them. Megan stepped closer, blocking any further access into the room.

"Let him in."

Both girls swung around in confusion at Deb's soft command. "Deb, you don't owe him anything," Megan began, still not moving from her protective position.

"I know, but he deserves to meet his daughter. Can you guys give us a minute?"

"That's the Deb I remember, always wanting what I'm offering," Tucker sneered.

The sleezy look of triumph Tucker sent toward Frankie clearly made her blood simmer, her rage barely contained below the surface. She took a deep breath, attempting to gain control. "We'll be outside if you need us." At Deb's vacant nod, she closed the door, leaving it slightly ajar, just to be on the safe side.

"I don't like this. He's shonky as," Megan whispered.

"I'll be stuffed if I'm just going to leave Deb at his mercy. You stay here. I'm going to get Senhor Eduardo," Frankie declared as she stormed off.

Deb stood woodenly, her face blank as if she had not just overheard every word her friends had uttered. "What changed? Why do you want to see your daughter now?" she asked flatly. She was curiously numb to whatever his answer might be.

Tucker stepped forward, grabbing both of her upper arms insistently, a world of insincere regrets on full display. "I've made mistakes. A lot of them. But darlin', I realized that the best thing for you is to have me here."

"Oh."

He gripped her arms more tightly. "I think we need to do this for our daughter. I want to try and be a family. What do you think?"

The curiously numb feeling continued to hold Deb in its thrall, almost comforting in its embrace. "I think you should meet your daughter."

Senhor Eduardo barged into the room, Sra Ana, Frankie, Gabi, and Megan hot on his heels. He came to an abrupt halt as he sighted Tucker. "And you are the father? Am I right in guessing that?"

"Yeah, boy. I'm the one that knocked her up." He swaggered over, hand extended.

Senhor Eduardo looked coldly down, his mouth pursed in distaste. Leaving the proffered hand hanging, he stepped around him to Deb. "Do you want him here?"

"He's Grace's father," she replied robotically, not meeting his eye. "He'll probably be around a lot more getting to know her. Us."

Tucker smiled smugly at the outraged group. "Well, looks like we're all going to be one big happy family."

"Not on my bloody watch," Frankie raged.

The bronc rider crossed his arms arrogantly, a smarmy smirk marring his face. "Now, that's the thing, darlin'. It's not your watch, is it?"

Frankie looked as if she was set to swing a punch at him, Gabi and Megan only seconds behind her. Sra Ana put a restraining hand on Frankie's arm. Calmly, she looked Tucker up and down. "I am sure I would like to get to know you better. I think Deb once said your name was Tucker?" she queried, firmness in her eyes.

"Yeah, Tucker."

"Tucker, Senhor Eduardo and I are very fond of Deb and Grace." She stressed the very. "We would not take it kindly if you were to mistreat them."

Tucker pulled an unresisting Deb close to him. "She's worth a lot to me."

The girls shuddered in disgust, only making Tucker sneer more. "If we're done here, I've got places to be." Looking at Frankie's curled lip and wrinkled nose, he chuckled slyly. "But don't worry. I won't stay away long."

Deb watched him go, her face expressionless. "I don't want to hear whatever it is you all think I need to hear. He wants us to be a family. He thinks we should give us, I mean, our relationship, a second chance."

"Second chance!" exploded Frankie. "You guys didn't have a relationship! You had a bloody one-night stand!"

"Frankie," warned Megan.

"I think everyone needs to calm down," Gabi suggested, looking at her parents for support.

"I'm sorry I'm not perfect like you," Deb spat, venom dripping with each word. "What with your blooming perfect Luciano and your marriage. The bright shining star that graces us with your presence. But this is my life and you can butt out."

Frankie jerked back as if Deb had struck her, her hand flying to her mouth, hurt flaring in her eyes. "You can get stuffed, Deb. I bloody hope you know what you're doing for Grace's sake, but I want you to think about one thing. For someone who wants to be a family so much, he never even stuck around long enough to actually meet his daughter." She choked out the last words and flew out the door.

Deb turned cold eyes to the shocked group that remained. "If you have all said what you need to, I'm going to go lay down."

Mitch swerved, swearing in surprise as Frankie's truck hurtled past him on the Affinity Ranch drive, a hail of spraying rocks hitting his truck like bullets. *Stone the flaming crow, Frankie. What's got your panties up in a bunch?* The ranch was eerily empty as he pulled up. Even the horses seemed subdued. A prickle of apprehension ran up his spine. For a split second, he wondered if maybe Frankie was running away from something or someone.

Deciding he couldn't leave without making sure Deb and Gracie were safe, he determinedly marched to the bunkhouse. Inside, barely audible, he could make out soft baby noises, but otherwise, all was quiet. He knocked on the door, a feeling of unease still heavy in his stomach. When no answer was forthcoming, he checked the handle to see if it was unlocked and, finding it was, opened the door.

Baby Gracie was laying on her back on a brightly colored playmat underneath arches strung with toys. Deb stared at her vacantly from the couch. Distressingly, she gave no visible acknowledgement she was even aware of his presence. He cleared his throat.

"Hey, Deb. Everything okay here?"

She turned unblinking eyes to him. "Do you know how sick and tired I am of everyone always asking me that? It's not like anyone actually cares what the answer is, anyway. You all just need to start minding your own business."

For a moment, Mitch was struck by the thought that this wasn't Deb, but someone else in her body speaking. "I thought you were my business. You and Gracie."

Her expression seemed regretful for a moment, but it was gone before Mitch could even be sure he had seen it correctly. "Mitch, I can't be anything more than friends with you."

The floor dropped out from beneath him, all breath robbed from his lungs. "Why? What's changed?"

"Tucker was here. Grace's dad. He wants to be part of her life and he wants us to try and be a family."

"He can go take a flying leap," Mitch bellowed, the raw denial torn from his throat. Gracie gave a little cry at the harsh sound. He bent down to soothe her.

Deb swallowed, her hands twisting together, her eyes firmly on the floor. "Please don't make this any harder than it has to be. I owe it to him to do this."

Mitch shook his head in bewilderment. "You don't owe him anything. You don't owe me anything either, for that matter. But you sure as heck owe it to you and your little girl to think about this—*really* think about this."

Deb finally raised her eyes to meet his, tears shimmering

in them. It was oddly reassuring to see some emotion at least. "Please, Mitch," she pleaded. "I need to do this. I wish … it doesn't matter now." Her eyes dropped to the floor once again.

Mitch sunk down to his knees on the floorboards beside her. Gentle fingers tucked a strand of long hair behind her ear. Deb sucked in a frayed breath as he leaned in close.

"I think you're making a mistake." He wondered if she could feel the closeness of his lips, his breath warm on her ear. "No matter what happens. You need me, I'll be there." Loving lips brushed her forehead, lingering as if unwilling to end the moment. "Goodbye, Deb."

His touch set off a wave of emotions, regret rocketing through him. His anguish robbed him of his strength to rise to his feet, to leave her to the mercy of a man that didn't deserve her and Grace. At the soft click of the door closing, his façade crumbled under the weight of his loss, his heart ripped out and trampled on. As he walked away, head bowed low in grief, he could hear Grace blissfully fussing inside. Once inside the cab of his truck, Mitch buried his head in his hands and wept, his low sobs heartbroken.

CHAPTER 12

Megan stood, her hands clenched at her side, the slow burn of anger building as she watched the scene play out before her eyes. Deb stood, Grace held on one hip as Tucker patronized her every motion as she made him the cup of coffee exactly as he demanded. At last, he took a slurp and sprayed it over Deb, the hot liquid splashing on Grace. The baby gave a sharp cry of betrayal at the sudden pain, a new sensation. Tucker continued to berate her incompetence, wagging a finger in her face. Unable to take it anymore, Megan marched over and placed herself squarely in front of her friend.

"Enough!" she roared. Stunned silence broke out.

"I'm sorry you had to witness that," Tucker said, shocking Megan momentarily at the thought that he had given in so easily and admitted to his unacceptable behavior. It didn't last long. "Deb's incompetence got the baby hurt."

The blood began to pound in Megan's ears. She lifted her lip in a snarl. "Get out," she spat.

"Easy, darlin'."

"Don't patronize me. I'm not your *darlin'*. From where I'm

standing, you aren't even fit to breathe the same air as Deb and this baby. So. Get. Out!"

Tucker cocked his head, his hands spread wide in insincere regret. "Deb doesn't want me to go. In fact, she wants me to stay right here. Permanently." He smirked back at Megan as he patted Deb on the shoulder. Deb hung her head, not meeting Megan's eye. "Go ahead and tell her, darlin'."

"I want him to stay. Grace needs her father around, especially since I'm not capable of looking after her," Deb said quietly, speaking to her feet.

Megan's mouth gaped wide in disbelief. "Who says you aren't capable?" she asked, astonished.

"Tucker is the only one who understands. I need him to stay."

Megan wanted to grind her teeth in frustration. "I don't care what crap this is," she said to Tucker, gesturing at Deb. "But you remember—I'm watching, Tucker. There's a lot of people who care about Deb and that baby, and if they have anything to say about it—and I'm pretty sure they have a bloody lot to say about it—you won't be smirking for much longer."

"I think you'll find I'm not going anywhere."

"We'll see." Megan promised, eyeballing him as she settled back on the couch.

Senhor Eduardo stood despondently on the porch, staring morosely toward the barn and, more specifically, the bunkhouse. "He's no good," he grumbled. "I feel it in my bones."

"What you feel is the aches and pains of an old bull rider," Sra Ana said, sedately sipping her coffee. "He probably is no good, but Deb needs to decide that for herself."

"I am worried about her. Lately, she does not seem

herself. I will make him go," Senhor Eduardo decided, pleased to have finally come to a decision about the interloper.

"You can't. If you tell him to go, she will go with him and take our Grace with her. Then who will look out for them? At least we can keep an eye on things here, be here for her, keep her safe. She has Megan, Frankie and Gabriella."

Senhor Eduardo looked sourly at his wife. She returned his look, smiling calmly. "I hate it when you talk sense."

"I know."

"As soon as Deb comes to her senses, I get to kick him off this ranch."

"I will even help you put your boots on," Sra Ana promised. "Now, sit down and have one of these lamingtons. I used Frankie's recipe."

The slamming of the door echoed through the bunkhouse. Deb was grateful Megan had already left for the morning stables. Shame filled her at the thought of her friend witnessing yet another altercation between her and Tucker. Deb, who had always been strong and feisty, was so weakened by the toxic relationship with Tucker that she constantly questioned and berated herself. It was a case of crawling through each hour, each day, until bedtime would buy her some relief. Her brain tortured her with the same thoughts on repeat. That she wasn't good enough to be Grace's mother. That she was going crazy. Every day, she woke drenched in sweat. Her weight plummeted. She didn't want to die, but she didn't want to live either.

"Mommy's trying so hard," she whispered woefully to her daughter. "I just don't know what to do anymore. I feel like my head is filled with sawdust. I used to love working with the horses and now I dread I'll have to start helping again soon and they'll see how useless I am." Grace gurgled at her mother, earnestly trying to get her fist into her mouth. Tears flowed down Deb's bleak face. "Tucker is doing his best to help us. He's right. I'm being ungrateful. He could be on the road competing if he didn't have to stay here and keep an eye on me. I'm no good to anyone. But Mommy loves you."

Megan viciously stabbed at the straw bedding, pretending it was that bloody Tucker. No matter how she tried to show Deb that he was no good, her friend still clung to him as surely as a drowning man to a life raft. Try as she might, she couldn't see any sign of her once funny, confident friend.

"I said I would get you your money." Megan's ears pricked up at the hushed sound of Tucker's muffled conversation. "Don't worry about that. Me not competing isn't an issue anymore." She peered over the stall wall, trying to see where Tucker was. She ducked back down when she sighted him near the feed room. Holding her breath, she prayed he hadn't seen her. "I've found a golden goose, so to speak. And she'll give me whatever I ask for. All I need is a few more weeks and I'll have all your money."

Megan's mind raced as she digested the conversation she had just overheard. Deb would be devastated when she told her, but at least Tucker would be out of everyone's lives. Hopefully, once and for all.

CHAPTER 13

The forlorn clang of the farrier's hammer hitting metal matched the mood that gripped Mitch's heart as it rang out. The last nail hit home, and he lowered the horse's leg with a frustrated sigh.

"My friend, I would ask why so glum, but I think I know what, or should I say who, the problem is," Luciano said from where he held the horse's head.

"I don't understand why she is giving that bludging dipstick a chance. It's like she has a few sheep loose in the top paddock at the moment."

"Frankie is still on the road, sulking about what Deb said to her. But I know she is worried."

The rattle of a horse trailer captured both men's attention as Joao's truck pulled up. Luciano's face brightened. "Since you are nearly finished, why not stay? Joao and I are going to do some roping. Are you any good?"

"I don't want to blow my own horn, but I'm pretty handy," Mitch said modestly, packing his tools away. "Showing you fellas how a boy from the bush does it beats drinking with the flies."

Joao joined the conversation, a disgruntled expression on his face. "You give the flies a drink?"

"Nah, mate. That would be bloody stupid. It's when you drink alone. Enough of this yabbering. Do you wanna rope or not?"

The alcohol temporarily dulled the pain. Lately, it was the only thing that gave Mitch some quiet from the constant ache in his chest. It had been a good afternoon riding with the Brazilian boys. He'd forgotten how much he missed hanging out with his mates back home, catching up over a cold beer.

"Another one?" Luciano asked, offering up a beer.

"A fella's not a camel."

Luciano blinked. "I guess he isn't." He handed the drink over.

"Fair dinkum, he's a straight up mongrel," Mitch blurted angrily.

"We are speaking of Tucker?" Joao asked, hesitantly.

"What I really want to do is bail him up and make him leave her alone," Mitch continued.

"After what he did to my Querida, I am not so fond of him myself," Luciano agreed.

"At least you had the pleasure of giving him a good flogging."

Luciano cracked his knuckles, the sound unpleasantly reminiscent of breaking bones. "I would happily do it again."

"If you like, I can make him disappear. No one will ever find him again. I know some people that will even send you a video of him suffering before the end." Stunned silence greeted Joao's unexpected revelation.

Mitch laughed, slapping his knee. "That's funny as all get.

You're the last bloke I would expect to be able to make someone cark it."

Joao smiled modestly. "I have contacts back home."

"Does Senhor Eduardo know what sort of man is making puppy dog eyes at his daughter?" Luciano chuckled. "Maybe if Gabi knows this, she would be more interested." He slapped his friend on the shoulder. Joao smiled bashfully.

"Maybe we shouldn't knock him off," Mitch decided. A flash of inspiration came over him, burning the numbness away. "How much to just kneecap him?"

It was as if Deb watched from the outside, a stranger in her own body as she listlessly changed Grace's nappy. She was lethargic in her movements, a nameless trance still holding her in its sway. Even Megan's surprise appearance wasn't enough to shake her from its grip as she finished and picked her baby up.

"Deb, I need to talk to you."

"Anything you say to her, you can say in front of me," a male voice condescendingly responded. Tucker's large frame filled the doorway—the only way out of the nursery.

"Deb, I know Sra Ana would like to have a visit with Grace. Why don't we head over there and have a cuppa?" Megan suggested, her expression tightening with desperation, her eyes wide as if trying to send a message.

Tucker didn't move from the door, crossing his arms over his chest. "Deb isn't going anywhere. At least not with my daughter."

Megan's mouth fell open and she shot a look towards Deb. But Megan didn't understand, she didn't understand that she couldn't go anywhere without Tucker. She would never be able to comprehend how terrified she was of hurting Grace without him there.

"Deb, I know you're somewhere in there and I sure as heck need you right about now." She grabbed Deb's hand and tried to pull her forward. "We're leaving, all of us." But Deb remained still, as if her feet were embedded in concrete.

Tucker smirked at Megan. "I told you they weren't going anywhere," he sneered. "Isn't that right, darlin'?"

"Megan, I'm staying here with Tucker. We're a family," Deb said in a flat monotone.

"Deb, you don't mean that. He's only using you. Can't you see that?" Megan pleaded. "He's broke and he somehow owes someone money. He thinks you'll give it to him."

How could Megan even suggest such a thing? Of course Tucker couldn't have another motive, Deb didn't have the money to give, so how could that even be possible? "I don't believe you. Tucker is here for us."

"You need to shut up and mind your own business," Tucker threatened, taking a step into the room.

"Look at him, Deb. He's scared 'cause he knows I'm telling the truth." Megan's voice grew stronger.

"I said shut up!" Tucker roared. He picked up the carved cradle and threw it against the wall. It shattered on impact.

"What the bloody heck is going on here?"

Mitch's voice jolted through Deb and she couldn't find any words as the scene quickly played out before her. Mitch rushed into the room, grappling with Tucker. His balled fist collided with his nemesis's cheekbone, snapping his head back. Tucker stumbled, nearly falling over. Mitch grabbed his opponent by the shirt and heaved him to his feet, bringing his fist to Tucker's face, snapping his nose in a grotesque fashion. Satisfaction flared on Mitch's face as Tucker tried to defend himself, but his movements were too slow. Realizing he had beaten him, Mitch threw him away in disgust.

Deb dropped to her knees, Grace safely in her arms, beside the broken pieces of the cradle. Her last remaining thread of strength frayed before snapping completely, sending her plummeting over the edge and into the darkness. Hysterical sobs shook her thin frame, threatening to tear her apart from inside. She fought to reclaim control over her body, shocked by the sounds escaping from deep inside her chest. Deb picked up a fragment of carved wood, feeling the love and care Mitch had put into each etching he had made.

"Did you ever want to be a real family?" she asked brokenly.

For a frozen second, no one moved. Tucker's eyes flickered wildly to Deb before false bravado took hold and he sneered in disgust. "Did you ever believe I would want to be with a nutcase like you? I mean, look at you."

Mitch shook him angrily. "You don't talk to her like that!" Tucker fell silent.

"Is what Megan said true?" she asked softly. "Was it only because you wanted money?"

"You were nothing but a shag—and a lousy one at that— and then you had to go and get knocked up. No way was I going to have anything to do with that mess, but that was when I thought you only worked here, not owned part of it."

Deb's skin crawled at the smug smile he sent her way. "The jokes on you. I might be part owner, but we aren't making any money yet. We're still in the setup phase."

"This ranch must be worth a pretty penny," he suggested, casting his eye about.

Deb laughed hollowly. "I don't have a brass razoo. This ranch belongs to Gabi's father and we rent the space off him. All legit-like. Probably so maggoty scum like you don't get your hands on it. I think it's time for you to leave now."

"This isn't over. Not by a long shot. I'll get my money one way or anoth—" His last word was cut short by Mitch thumping him in the mouth with a resounding right hook. Bleeding, he stumbled from the room with Mitch hot on his heels.

Deb remained broken among the fragments. Megan settled beside her and gently took Grace, placing an arm around her. "He never wanted us."

Megan looked sadly at her. "No." Deb let her friend hold her as she sobbed out her pain. In Megan's arms, Grace smiled at her mother, the only bright light in the otherwise dark room.

~

"Is she okay?" Mitch asked, concern threading his voice.

"She's watching over Grace while she sleeps. If you want, I think it would be okay for you to go in," Megan suggested.

Mitch softly padded across the room to the nursery. As he entered, a gentle glow illuminated Deb's features, making them appear almost angelic as she kept vigil over her daughter, now in a portacot after the demolition of the cradle.

"I'm sorry about the cradle. I'm sure Tucker didn't know what he was doing," she said quietly.

Mitch bit down hard on the sharp flare of anger that rocketed through his body at her words. "I'm dead certain he knew exactly what he was doing. What I can't figure out is why you're bloody defending him, especially after tonight." Mitch was devastated as Deb raised shame-filled eyes to meet his. A need stronger than anything he had ever experienced surged through him. This wasn't right. This was his family. He needed to protect them.

"I just feel mixed up inside. Some days, I don't even feel like myself. It's like I'm watching someone else live my life. I know that doesn't make sense," she admitted sadly. "I feel like I'm slowly going crazy. Tucker says I'm mental."

"Tucker's a jerk. Maybe there is something wrong, but I would listen to someone that bloody knows what they're talking about. Have you talked to a doctor about this?"

"I'm scared they'll tell me I actually am crazy," she said, her head still bowed. Shame and fear laced her words.

"All I know is you deserve more than this. The thoughts in your head, Tucker treating you like this. You're worth more. Actually, you're worth everything." He yearned to reach out and touch her, to somehow physically show her.

Deb gave a hollow little laugh. "Right now, I don't feel like I'm worth anything. I'm so broken."

Unable to hold himself back, Mitch wrapped his arms around Deb, holding her close in an attempt to take away some of her pain. "If you won't do it for yourself, do it for your baby girl." A raw intensity flowed out of him with his words.

"That's not fair. You know I'd do anything for her," she protested, some vigor surprising them both with its sudden appearance.

Mitch smiled. "That's my girl. If you don't feel strong enough right now, how about we do it together? Just until you're back to your formidable self again."

Deb gave him a tired look. "I'd like that." She snuggled into his arms a little more. "I'd like that a bloody lot."

CHAPTER 14

*D*eb nestled on the couch, blanket pulled around her, feeling marvelously spoiled. Mitch lay on the floor playing with Grace as she tried to roll from her tummy to her back. The cozy domestic scene was one that felt surprisingly right. The last week had been one of hard soul searching. In a way, it had been a relief to hear the doctor say that she wasn't crazy, but in fact had postnatal depression. Deb had been embarrassed by the prescription of medication and weekly psychologist visits, but Mitch had been quick to reassure her that no one would think less of her.

Just thinking about her friends was enough to make Deb feel deeply ashamed of the way she'd treated them. She still hadn't been able to pick up the phone and call Frankie to apologize. She wasn't even sure her friend would answer the phone. And honestly, she didn't blame her. Megan had offered to talk to Frankie and clear it all up, but Deb felt she owed it to them both to cowgirl up and do it herself. But therein lies the dilemma. She hadn't yet found the courage to actually do it.

A gentle knock on the door startled her from her somber reflections in her blanket cocoon. As if her thoughts had come to life, Frankie awkwardly stood on the threshold, uncertainly holding a packet of Tim Tams. She nervously cleared her throat.

"Um, is it okay if I come in?"

Deb sat paralyzed, dreading the confrontation she was sure was about to come. Mitch scooped Grace up in his arms and gave Frankie a welcoming hug. Her daughter giggled as Frankie blew a raspberry on her cheek.

"Hello, Gracie. You've grown." She winced as long strands of hair were caught in chubby baby hands. Apprehensively, she looked over at Deb as she untangled herself from the strong grip. "Hello, Deb."

Mitch looked between the women. "Well, I'm going to take this little tacker to visit the Cabrera's. Sra Ana mentioned something about cake." Deb couldn't believe it! He was actually going to desert her in her hour of need. "Play nice, girls." The awkward silence stretched out uncomfortably as he closed the door on his retreating back.

The plastic wrapper of the Tim Tam packet crinkled as Frankie nervously gripped it. She thrust them toward Deb. "I got you these."

Deb put her hands up to take the packet, worried that if she didn't, Frankie was liable to take out an eye. "Thanks."

Frankie plonked down beside her friend in frustrated defeat, trapping Deb by sitting on the blanket. "This is stupid."

"Yeah."

"I'm sorry," Frankie said.

Deb couldn't believe her ears. Why on earth would Frankie be sorry? It was her who had stuffed everything up. "Frankie, I'm the one that treated you like crap."

"No, Deb. You were hurting. I just couldn't see it at the time. I should have been here for you."

Tears welled up as Deb fought her shame. How could she

deserve a friend like this? "I don't know if I would have let you anyway. You had a lot going on, too."

"Yeah, but none of it was more important to me than you. If you had needed me, if I had known you needed me, I would have dropped everything and come home." She earnestly took her friend's hand. "I know I'm a bit late to the party, but I'm here now. Do you want to talk about it?"

Deb sorted through her emotions, the words still hard to come by even though the last week had brought her some clarity. A sadness darkened her face. "I used to think I was this strong, capable cowgirl. Now I can't even remember who that girl was." There was a brokenness to her words, a fragility that still threatened to crumple her soul into nothingness.

Frankie gave her hand a reassuring squeeze. "Well I can tell you plenty of good yarns about what sort of girl she was. I remember this one time at a B&S Ball, she decided to put plastic snakes in all of the swags."

Deb chuckled. "Dang, that was funny. All those grown men screaming like bloody little girls."

"What do you need from me? To help get the Deb we all love back?"

"I think maybe not let me get lost so much in myself. Not let me push you away. The medication helps—it kinda clears the fog. Talking about it, especially with the shrink, is hard but good, if that makes sense? Kinda like going for a wax. You dread going, it hurts like all heck, but afterwards, you like the results."

"I think I can do that." Frankie said. "Now, these Tim Tams aren't going to eat themselves. Do you want me to put the kettle on?"

"Yes, but on one condition."

"Anything."

"Get your butt up, so I can free myself from this darn blanket."

The suds swirled over work-calloused hands, mesmerizing Deb as she watched Mitch wash up in the kitchen sink. "I can't believe you actually volunteered to change a nappy."

"I'm a big tough bloke. I can handle a nappy change."

"Then what was with all of the retching and gagging noises I heard?" she challenged, mirth twitching at the corners of her mouth.

"I said I could handle it. I didn't say I could handle it quietly. For such a cute little thing, she sure can produce some stinky poo." He reached for the towel and began drying his hands. He looked up at Deb, his expression serious as he gently touched her face. "It's good to see you smile, even if it is at my expense."

The urge to nuzzle into the warmth of his hand surprised Deb. "It's good to want to smile again." Mitch stepped back, leaning his weight against the kitchen counter, the sudden loss of contact leaving her feeling bereft.

"So, I take it you and Frankie are mates again?"

"Yeah, I think we always were. I was just too blind to see there wasn't anything I could do that would make her hate me. She's a good friend, probably better than I deserve," she admitted.

"To your friends, you're worth it." He hesitated, as if questioning the timing of his next words. "To me, you're worth it."

She smiled at him warmly. "I'm blessed to have you all as my friends. I honestly don't know what I would have done without you all these last few weeks."

"I said I would always be here for you and I meant every word." As if frightened that he would lose his nerve, he rushed on. "I love you, Deb."

Deb's eyes widened at his words. "I, ah, love you, too. You're one of my best friends."

Mitch gave a long sigh, apparently coming to a decision, a determined glint in his eyes. "I'm just going to bloody well say this. I love you, and not just as a friend. I'll wait for you to be ready if that's what you need from me, but I want more. I dream of being lucky enough to have more with you."

She let out her breath, not even aware she had been holding it. A feeling, comforting in its warmth, filled her heart before it was chased away by regret. "I'm not in that place yet, to be more than friends. I need to put myself and my daughter first. In fact, a very smart fella once told me to do exactly that. And he was right, I need to get better and find me again before I can even think about having a relationship."

Mitch nodded. "I'm not going to give up on having an us one day. But I'll take being friends. I just want to be part of your lives."

Gratitude filled Deb that she hadn't driven him away. Now the disaster had been averted, she didn't know what she would have done if she'd lost his friendship. Thankfully, she hadn't had to find out.

*L*ike a flower blooming after a long hard winter, Deb finally began to live again. Gradually, she cried less and smiled more. Or, at least, that's what it felt like as she strapped on the baby carrier. Grace chirruped happily, and Deb smiled as she kissed her head and wondered how long her little girl would still have the sweet smell of babyhood.

"Well, look what the cat dragged in," greeted Megan. "Do you even know which end of the pitchfork to hold anymore?"

"Oh, so funny. Did you think of that all by yourself?" Deb retorted tartly before laughing loudly, joyous to be out in the sunshine again with the horses and her friends.

"Yeah, Megan's writing all of her own material these days," Frankie said, joining them. "Hey, gorgeous girl," she said as she tickled Grace's cheek. "You gonna make sure Mommy does a good job?"

"I can run rings around you guys, even on my worst days," Deb said, grabbing a wheelbarrow and heading to the first stall."

"Hey, Deb?" Megan called.

"Yeah?"

"It's good to have you back."

Deb breathed in deeply, pungent fragrances of horse manure, straw and shavings once again feeling familiar. Her world was right again. She was finally home. "It's good to be back."

"Frankie, Megan, are you in here?" called Gabi, her voice echoing through the barn.

Megan popped her head from the stall she was cleaning as Deb stepped onto the top of the stairs, baby monitor in hand.

"Yeah, we even have Deb gracing us with her presence today. Frankie's training in the arena if you're chasing her as well," Megan said.

"That's okay, she can meet my brother later."

"Sorry, I just had to put Grace down for a nap. But as long as I stay in the barn, I can get reception." She looked at the stranger beside Gabi. "What did I miss?"

"I was just about to introduce my brother, Carlos, to Megan and now you." She smiled proudly up at her brother. "Carlos, these are my business partners and friends, Megan and Deb. I will introduce you to Frankie when she comes back in."

She looked curiously at the tall dark-haired man who ambled alongside Gabi. Even with the stone-colored Stetson and aviator sunglasses, the resemblance to Gabi was unmistakable.

Megan stepped forward, wiping her dirty hands on the leg of her jeans. "Nice to meet the mysterious brother we hear so much about but never see."

Carlos took his sunglasses off. He had deep dark-brown eyes, almost verging on black, Deb noted, before he engulfed her hand in his much larger one. There was a pleasant firmness to his grip as he smiled at her in greeting.

"I hope I have a chance to defend myself from anything they have said about me in my absence."

Gabi playfully smacked her brother on the shoulder. "We have said nothing but the truth. I can't help if you were such a terrible big brother growing up. You and Joao were always running off and leaving me behind."

"I'd say it's more like you running off and leaving Joao behind these days. Or maybe you like him chasing after you." Carlos teased, a knowing look in his eye.

Gabi blushed a brilliant shade of crimson. "That's not true. He's just a family friend. Anyway, he's your best friend."

"What does that have to do with him chasing you?" he said, arching an eyebrow at her. "Would you like my blessing? 'Cause if that's all you're waiting for, you've got it. He's a great guy. I don't know why he would put up with you."

Megan and Frankie both laughed. It was obvious from their teasing that they loved each other, but she wouldn't expect anything less from the Cabrera's. Gabi's expression suddenly turned to pure business.

"Megan, are you able to bring Delila in? This big lug here is going to scan her and see if we have a little Sampson baby growing in there."

"Sure thing." Megan grabbed a halter and lead from the wall hook. "I can't wait to have some foals start hitting the ground. Foaling season was always my favorite part of working at the stud back home."

"I'm glad you feel that way. Are you able to stay about and help my brother with anything he needs?"

"I'm sure she will be more than happy to take care of any needs he might have." Deb gave Megan a wink.

Megan turned the exact shade of red Gabi had displayed only moments earlier. "Right, I'm going to go get Delila then." She spun on her heel and left Deb enjoying her attempt at wit. "And I said I missed the old Deb! What was I thinking?" she muttered mutinously.

~

Deb looked around at her friends jubilantly celebrating the confirmation that Delila carried a very precious Sampson baby. "Gosh, imagine in a few years I could be competing on both father and offspring," Frankie said in amazement to Gabi. "It's hard to believe."

"You making your career first on Delila, then Sampson, and then on their offspring is marketing gold," Gabi responded astutely, her business mind already ticking over with the possibilities.

"I don't care as long as I get to be there for the foaling," Megan added. "Today reminded me how much I like working with the broodmares and foals."

"Not to mention cute vets," Deb noted slyly.

"That's not true," Megan argued. She looked apologetically at Gabi. "I mean, your brother is obviously not ugly. Deb's twisting my words again. Frankie, make her stop!"

"I'll play nice," Deb promised, chuckling. "But there's something to what Megan was saying."

Megan's brow wrinkled. "That you're always twisting my words?"

"No, well I mean, I do, but that wasn't what I was getting at. I've been thinking a lot about where I see my future lately."

"She's going to say she's leaving us, isn't she?" Gabi assumed. "You can't leave."

"Why would you want to leave us?" Frankie wailed, dramatically slumping back against the cushions of the couch.

"I'll finally get some bloody peace and quiet," Megan grumbled.

Deb held her hand up for silence. "First of all, I'm not going anywhere. And second of all, you'd miss me, Megan," she said, looking pointedly at her friend.

"A girl can dream," Megan retorted.

"I'm confused. Why did you say you were leaving then?" Frankie said.

Deb sighed. She loved her friends dearly, but sometimes, they really were hard work. "I never said I was leaving, you guys presumed that. Which, to be honest, was kinda hurtful." She assumed a wounded expression. "Especially given my fragile mental state." She looked at the serious, worried faces that greeted her announcement. "Too soon?"

"Most definitely too soon," Frankie declared flatly.

"Anyway, where was I before you all so rudely interrupted?" Deb paused to gather her thoughts. "That's right. Where I see my future. Since we moved over here, I've just been kinda going with the flow. But since I've had Grace, I don't want to ride the young horses anymore. I can't risk coming off and getting hurt."

Frankie looked ashamed. "I'm so sorry that I didn't think of it. It wasn't fair to assume you would come back and want to keep doing it, you know, once you felt better."

"I wouldn't have thought I would feel that way either till I had Gracie."

Gabi chewed her lip thoughtfully. "Megan, I know we keep asking this of you, but would you be able to continue keeping the horses in work when Frankie is away? At least for the time being. I know Frankie promised we would find someone to help, and I swear we will. But with everything that's been going on, it kinda got put on the backburner."

"I can, but not if I'm still doing the stable stuff as well. It's just too much. Plus, long term, I don't see myself working the horses," Megan replied.

Gabi looked to Deb. "It might be best to split roles as the stud gets bigger anyway. So, if we made you Barn Manager and you looked after the day-to-day aspect of managing the horses"—she glanced at Megan—"and you just looked after keeping the horses in work, would everyone be happy? At least for the time being?"

"Happy as a pig in mud," both Megan and Deb said in unison.

"I need to get out and meet more people," Megan said sourly. "I'm even starting to sound like her."

Deb thumped her on the back heartily. "Can't help it if my awesomeness is starting to rub off."

"Awesomeness wasn't the word I was going for."

"Speaking of awesomeness, how was working with the spunky Carlos?"

Megan gave her a look of disgust. "He was a perfect gentleman. Very professional."

"That's a shame," Deb said, giving her a sympathetic look. "Maybe next time, you can get him to forget he's a gentleman."

"Are you two just going to sit there giggling or are you going to help?" Megan asked her chuckling friends.

"When she's teasing you, she's leaving us alone," Frankie said, obviously enjoying her discomfort. "Plus, I still remember how much you enjoyed it when she was giving it to me. Karma."

"I need to get new friends." Megan threw a cushion Frankie's way.

Deb watched the interplay between her friends, grateful to once again feel like she was part of the tight bond they all shared. Sometimes miracles did happen.

CHAPTER 16

Deb smiled as she waved goodbye to Mitch, his truck rattling over the bumps in the drive. "You really should do something about that," Megan said. "You know, now that you're the Barn Manager and all."

"I'll add it to my list. I swear you've bloody taken almost childish delight in adding to my list of chores." Deb looked down at the monitor, her child still slumbering peacefully on the screen. "Was there anything in particular you wanted, or did you just come to give me an earbashing?"

"Just wanted to say hi to Mitch before he left, but I see I'm too late. Not that I think he cares that much with you keeping him company. Did you ask him about those new shoes for Sampson?"

"He said he doesn't think they'll make any difference. He just put the same type he always has on," Deb said.

"Cool, I'll let Frankie know. So, everything is good with you guys?"

"Yeah, as good as we ever were. Which is great, I guess."

Deb was at a loss to explain how she felt. She was grateful Mitch still wanted to have anything to do with her after everything that had happened, let alone to still be her friend.

But lately, she found herself remembering how safe she had felt in his arms. No, it was more than that. She felt cherished.

Megan looked intently at her friend. "What's going on in that noggin of yours?"

"Maybe I've backed myself into a corner."

"With Mitch?"

"Yeah. I think I like him."

"About bloody time you admitted it to yourself. So, how did he take it when you told him?

"I haven't told him."

"Ah, why?"

"I haven't exactly been making the best life choices lately. How do I know this isn't another mistake?"

"Because it's Mitch, for bloody sakes," Megan exclaimed. "You're crazy if you let him get away." She crossed her arms over her chest. "Look, I'll admit I was jealous when he started showing you attention, but I was never in with a chance. You guys were always meant to be together. He loves you, and he loves that little girl of yours." Megan blinked rapidly. "I must have some dust or something in my eyes."

"Aw, come here you big softie." Deb pulled the resisting Megan into a bear hug. "It means a lot, you saying that."

"Well, don't make me regret saying it to you. Go catch your cowboy."

"Hello," Mitch's voice came through the phone.

"Hi, it's Deb," she said nervously, immediately feeling like an idiot.

"I know. I have your name saved in my phone as Gracie's mom," he said, amused.

Deb was taken aback in surprise. "Do you really?"

"Fair dinkum. Do you reckon I would joke about something like that?"

"That's actually really sweet."

"I'm a sweet kinda bloke. Didn't you realize?"

"Ah, anyway, I was calling to see if maybe you would like to do something with me and Grace," she said hesitantly, feeling sick as she battled with the anxiety rising up within.

"Like a date?"

"I mean, it doesn't have to be."

"I'm just teasing. I would love to go on a date with my two favorite ladies. Tell you what, how about I make us a picnic lunch and we can go somewhere nice? You just pick a day and time and I'll make it happen."

Relief made Deb let her breath out with an audible whoosh. She was fairly certain it was loud enough for Mitch to hear on the other end of the phone. "That sounds good. How about Saturday?"

"I've cleared my entire day. Now, don't eat a big breakfast. I'm going to make you girls a feast."

As Deb hung up the phone, a pleasant flutter of anticipation danced in her belly. Maybe she wasn't making a mistake after all.

Mitch gallantly offered his arm as he settled both of them into his truck, fussing to make sure the baby capsule was properly secured. On the drive to the secret picnic location that no amount of prodding had been able to pry from him, the conversation flowed easily and comfortably between them. Grace gurgled and chattered, happy to be in the midst of them. It came as a surprise when the truck came to a halt. Deb peered curiously outside to discover they had pulled into the botanical gardens. She gaped at Mitch in astonishment.

"This is literally the last place I thought you would bring us today and yet, it's kinda perfect."

"I try," he said humbly. "Now, my ladies, shall we proceed and find a prime location to lay out our feast?" Grace giggled happily up at him. "That's a yes from the little cowgirl." He stared intently at Deb. "And what about her beautiful mom?"

Deb gave him a smile, her happiness radiating from her. "I couldn't imagine being anywhere else today."

He blinked as if blinded by the brightness that shone from her. For a moment, it appeared as if he was going to say something, a look of intense yearning naked in his eyes, before he changed his mind. Giving a rueful little shake of his head, he smiled. "I think I know where we should head."

They walked past carefree butterflies that fluttered from flower to flower, their only care the next bloom upon which to land in the warm sunshine. Deb envied their jauntiness, thinking that, if she could somehow find a way to bottle it, she would be a millionaire. Grace was fascinated by the reflections on the water in the gardens, the willows kissing the surface like lost lovers as they crossed the arched wooden bridge. At last, Mitch selected a spot on the green parklands under a shady elm.

"This, fittingly, is called The Horseshoe," he said by way of explanation as he set the picnic basket down and proceeded to spread out the rug. Deb gently lowered Grace to the ground, her daughter immediately reaching to grab handfuls of the lush grass.

Deb watched in awe at the mountain of food containers he emptied from the wicker basket. "How on earth did you fit all of that in there?" she blurted out. "And more importantly, did you actually make all of this?"

Mitch looked guiltily at her. "I would like to say, as a disclaimer, that I was in the kitchen throughout the cooking and baking process for each and every item." He held out his hand to show her a red painful-looking blister on the back of his hand. "I bloody well burnt myself on the oven getting the sausage rolls out and all Frankie could do was laugh," he said indignantly.

Enlightenment flared. "So, Frankie made this?"

"She let me stir some things and wash up," he confessed. "I just wanted it to be perfect and, well, I didn't think Vegemite sandwiches were gonna cut it."

Overcome by the sheer amount of care and effort he had put into arranging the perfect day for them, tears began to well up in Deb's eyes. Attempting to hide them, she ducked her head on the pretense of pulling some grass from Grace's hand before it could find its way into her mouth. Fingers made coarse from work lifted her chin up gently as if she were made from the finest china.

"I didn't mean to make you cry. I deadset just wanted to make you happy. That's pretty much all I've wanted for a long time now." His voice was gruff from emotion.

She sniffled. "These are happy tears." She shrugged, her face turning sad. "I just can't remember anyone ever going to so much effort for me."

He tenderly wiped the tears from her eyes. "Then you had better get used to it. I plan on doing it often, if you'll let me."

Her heart lurched at the emotion in his voice. "I think I'd like that," she said softly. Feeling as if she had finally climbed her way out of the dark, hope blossomed within her. Maybe she could have her happy ever after, after all.

Deb closed the door gingerly behind her, the click of the door barely audible. "I think we plumb tuckered her out," she whispered.

"I think she had fun," Mitch whispered back.

"So do I." A calm happiness glowed from her. "I had fun, too."

"Then my work here is done."

Mitch reached for her hand as they walked toward the door, the sweet gesture making Deb's belly flip-flop. "Thank you for everything today. It meant a lot to me."

"I want to say something smooth and cool, but I'm just a bloke from the bush. So, I'm going to tell you how it is. I love you, and I love that little girl in there, and you know it. I'm hoping I'm not reading the signals wrong here. Do you want more? You know, more than just friends?" He looked down at their joined hands as if embarrassed at his outburst.

Deb's heart twisted in her chest, love gripping her for this man who stood before her who had never once given up on her. "I love you, too."

His eyes widened at her words, a slow beatific smile stealing across his features. "Strewth, I never thought I would live to see the day that you, Deb Burke, actually admitted you love me." His smile turned mischievous. "But you're only human, after all, and can't fight my charms forever, I guess."

Deb gave an unladylike snort. "So humble."

His expression turned serious, somehow at odds with his usual larrikin expression. "Tonight, you've humbled me. I won't ever take those words you said for granted." His eyes never once leaving her face, he gently cupped her chin with his fingers, bringing her lips to meet his. Deb closed her eyes, losing herself to everything but the feeling of his skin against hers. As he pulled back, she slowly opened them, already mourning the moment that had passed. "I think I had better leave on that note. You need to get some sleep, young lady."

Deb laughed. "Only if Grace got the memo."

"Make sure you thank Megan and Gabi for making themselves scarce too," he wryly observed.

"Subtle, weren't they?" She yawned.

"Good night, Deb. Love you."

"Love you, too."

Deb closed the door and leaned against it feeling giddy as a schoolgirl. Well. Well, indeed.

CHAPTER 17

There certainly was something to be said for waking up with a bubble of anticipation of what the day would bring. The effervescence of happiness from last night still fizzed away in Deb's heart. Who would have thought that Mitch, teasing little Mitch from Mrs Humprey's class, could put such a smile on her face and a flutter in her heart? She glanced down at the monitor, relieved to see Grace was still sleeping peacefully.

"Thanks for giving Mommy a chance for a coffee in peace."

Blessed silence greeted her in the kitchen, a note on the table from Megan and Gabi informing her the stables had been done for the day and they would be back from Frankie and Luciano's after lunch to hear all the juicy gossip from her date. Exuberance burst within her again, the smile on her face widening as she remembered the previous day. She stared, dreamy-eyed, as the kettle boiled. Checking that her daughter was still asleep, she blissfully walked down the stairs. It was too nice a morning to be cooped up inside. Caught up in fanciful thoughts, she barely glanced at her phone when it rang before answering it. Too late, she realized it was Tucker.

"What the bloody heck do you want?" she greeted him harshly, the bubble of happiness well and truly popped.

"Now, darlin', is that any way to greet your baby's daddy?" he contemptuously sneered thought the phone.

Deb gripped the phone tightly, fighting the urge to hang up. "What do you want?" she demanded in a no-nonsense voice. "I don't have time to deal with you today."

"I think you will make time. In fact, I can guarantee it."

Deb shivered at the unspoken threat evident in his words. "Just spit it out. Or are you planning on boring me to death with all your yabbering?"

"You'd wanna watch how you speak to me, Deb." The menace in his voice sent a trickle of apprehension dancing up her spine. "What I want is money. I don't even want that much. You and your rich friends should have no trouble coming up with a measly $50,000."

Deb struggled to contain the hysterical giggle that fought to escape her lips at the situation. "Mate, you've seen my bank accounts. I don't have that sort of money."

"You'll find it. If you want to keep Grace, you will."

The breath fled her lungs at his words. "You're not taking Grace from me. You don't even want her except as a way to get back at me," she cried frantically.

"You're right. I don't care about you at all. But I do care about money. Now, be a good little girl and make sure I get it."

"No judge would ever give you custody."

"That's where you're wrong. I have videos, lots of videos, from when you were all whacked. You really were a bad Mommy. If I take that to court, no way will they leave Grace with a freak show like you. I mean, even the doctors say you're crazy and have to take pills." A black abyss opened at Deb's feet, threatening to swallow her back down to the depths she had only recently crawled out from. "I'll take it from your silence that you agree to my terms. I'll be in touch with details of a drop off for the cash." The line went dead.

She threw the phone away from her with all the strength she still possessed. Seconds later, it hit her. A tidal wave of despair, head-spinning, heart-wrenching, stomach-curdling, knee-buckling desperation. Tears fell down Deb's ashen face as she struggled to draw in air. She battled against the panic, the tightening of her chest as if the muscles were trying not to let another breath in. Then a gasp forced its way in, shallow lungs unable to move against her heavy ribs, her mind static as she sunk against the wall.

"Deb, is it not a beautiful day?" Senhor Eduardo said, appearing around the corner. He stopped short at the sight of her chalky complexion and tear-stained cheeks. "What has happened? Is the baby okay?"

Her eyes clouded over. She raised them to meet his, her eyelashes spiked with the evidence of her despair. "Grace is fine, for now." Her voice sounded far away. "I just don't know what to do anymore, Senhor Eduardo. The more I try, the more I get knocked back down again. I'm just so tired."

Senhor Eduardo sat her down gently. "Life is a tiring journey. It's not for the faint-hearted."

"I don't think I can do this anymore," she blubbered, ashamed at her failure.

"You are strong. My own mae never thought she was strong. She never left her village. But she was the strongest person I have ever known. Getting through life with no scars is not strength, it is luck. Real strength comes from fighting, clawing at life until you bend it to your will. My mae, she had seven children to raise after my papai died. And she did it because she never cowered at life's feet." He handed her a handkerchief, his expression somber as he peered intently at her, searching for evidence she had heard him, or more than that, that she had understood his words.

Deb wiped her eyes and blew her nose. "I never was one of those delicate weepy women. I'm an ugly crier all the way."

"There is no shame in your emotions showing, Deb," he reassured her, giving her knee a squeeze. "Now, do you want to tell me what the cause of this is?"

"I will. But first, I need to get the others back here," she said determinedly, sitting taller as she came to a decision. "He can't break me if I'm not alone."

~

Her friends' faces ran the gamut of expressions, Frankie looked sickly horrified, her eyes wide with terror for the predicament Deb now found herself in. "Bloody heck, Deb."

Luciano stood stoically beside her. He looked meaningfully toward Joao. "Maybe it's time you call those people."

Mitch put an arm protectively around Deb. "The only way he's bloody getting his hands on Gracie is over my dead bloody body. He isn't taking her anywhere." Megan wordlessly left the room. Deb experienced a stab of hurt that her friend could so easily shrug her off in this hour of need.

Gabi decisively pulled her phone out of her pocket. "Let me call some people." She scurried from the room, closing the bedroom door behind her.

Megan re-entered the room holding a handgun like she meant business, a vengeful gleam in her eyes. "If he shows his face around here again, he can say hello to my little friend." She slapped the side of it meaningfully onto her palm for emphasis.

"Holy heck, Megan!" exclaimed Frankie, her mouth open in shock. "When did you start being a thug? And more importantly, where have you been hiding it?"

"Under my bed. I wanted to be able to protect us if we needed it." Deb was ashamed she had doubted her friend's loyalty, but more so that she had put her in a position that she had felt she needed to protect them and buy a gun.

Gabi strode triumphantly back into the room, a picture of satisfaction. "I think I might have a solution."

"Is it permanent?" Mitch asked.

"Not as permanent as Joao's, but probably more legal and he won't bother us again." She sat down, consulting the notes she had written. The friends leaned forward. "Okay, here's the plan…"

CHAPTER 18

The dive Mitch, Luciano and Joao entered was too decrepit to even deserve that title. Mitch's boots threatened to be sucked off by the sticky floor fighting him for possession of his footwear. Long before his eyes adjusted to the dim interior, his nostrils were assaulted with a horrific stench of rancid food, spoiled beer and stale cigarette smoke. Cobwebs hung like chandeliers from the ceiling, making him duck as he made his way forward toward the scarred and stained bar.

"Classy," Joao muttered, swatting an errant web from his hat.

"What can I get ya'll?" drawled the bartender, casting a lazily assessing eye over them.

"They're here to see me."

Tucker lounged in a corner booth, beer in hand. Mitch was impressed the man had the internal fortitude to swallow the brew from the cracked and chipped mug. Luciano looked at the others in distaste at the thought of joining him and touching any more of the furniture than was absolutely required. Mitch didn't blame him, grimacing as he parked himself gingerly down.

"Do you have it or what?" Tucker demanded, arrogance stamped over his face. "I must admit, I'm surprised you guys are playing Deb's errand boys, but I don't care as long as you got my money."

"I reckon a bloke like you is gonna be real popular in prison." Mitch leaned back, the leather backrest creaking in protest at the movement. "Don't you, fellas?"

Luciano smiled grimly. "I'm sure there are a lot in there that are more experienced than you at bareback riding. Will want to see if you can last the full eight seconds."

"Just give me the money," Tucker blustered. "I don't have time to listen to your garbage."

"It's not too late for me to make a phone call," appealed Joao. "We don't have to tell Gabi."

Luciano pursed his lips considering. "I do not have any secrets from my Querida, but I could make an exception for this."

Tucker's head swiveled like a spectator at the tennis as he followed the interplay between the men. "I don't know what the heck you guys are talking about, but I'm out of patience." He stood angrily. "Be sure to tell Deb that this is all your fault for jerking me around."

"I'd bloody sit if I was you," Mitch growled, slapping the table, a move he instantly regretted when his palm stuck to the clammy surface. His face must have clearly conveyed the threat as Tucker obediently dropped back into his seat. "Much better. Now, where was I? That's right, you going to prison."

"I ain't going nowhere."

"And if you are a good boy and do what you're told, then maybe you can avoid that. Now, Deb has friends, people that care about her. And they're real smart folks, too. Now I wouldn't expect you to understand what friends are like, being bloody unlikable and all, but where I come from, we all have each other's back." He rifled in his pocket and withdrew a large envelope. "I'm going to need you to sign these."

"Or what?" Tucker asked sullenly.

"Or I can give all of the messages Deb has from you to a judge. And these blokes here"—he gestured at Luciano and Joao—"are more than happy to testify what happened here today. See, these smart friends of Deb that I mentioned, they also have high-powered attorneys. And do you know what those attorneys reckon?" He spread his hands wide in question. With no forthcoming answer from the deathly silent cowboy across the table, Mitch lifted his hat and scratched his head in thought. "Now, I'm a fairly simple bloke and not familiar with all this legal jargon, so you fellas will have to correct me if I get anything wrong," he said to his friends. "But the gist of it was this. You've been a very naughty boy. And what you're trying to do to Deb, I believe they call that extortion. Luciano, can you jog my memory with what the punishment for that is?"

Luciano smiled grimly, a dark satisfaction gleaming. "Last I checked, fifteen years."

"Woah." Tucker held his hands up. "Now, easy there. No need to get hasty. Maybe we can come to some sort of arrangement. Maybe I was being too greedy with the $50,000. Look, tell Deb I'll take $10,000 and I'll even give her more time to get it."

Before Tucker could react, Mitch reached across the table and grabbed a handful of his shirt. "You bloody listen to me," he snarled, the anger rising off him like heat. "You're going to sign these bloody papers, and then you're going to get up outta here and Deb and that little girl that are too good for you, are never going to bloody hear from you again. If not, I'm going to open a can of trouble on your backside so big you're going to wish you went to prison. Do you understand me?" he ground out through clenched teeth. Tucker gulped. Judging by the difficulty he had in swallowing, it must have been one heck of a lump. Tucker nodded mutely. "Good, now does anyone have a pen?" Mitch said, releasing his shirt and calmly sitting down.

Joao held out a pen, disappointment plain in the down-turn of his mouth. "It's not too late for me to make a call."

"Maybe next time," Luciano offered to his downcast friend. "Who knows, maybe Gabi will have a use for your particular talents."

Joao visibly brightened at his words. "You think she would be impressed?"

"Anything's possible."

The words shimmered and blurred as Deb stared down at the paper, a fat teardrop splattering on the page.

"Hey!" exclaimed Gabi, whisking the document out of harm's way. "We need that to be legible, not all smeared."

"I can't believe it. It's like this weight was pressing down on me and now I can breathe again." She struggled to articulate the gift her friends had given her. Gratitude and love made the words thick in her throat. "How did you even know a lawyer to ask?"

"Oh, that was easy," Gabi said, dismissively waving her hand. "Bryce uses them all the time with his company, so I just called him and asked if he knew of a good one. He must send lots of work their way, 'cause I dropped his name and they wrote that document up in a jiffy, gave me instructions, and didn't charge me a dime."

"Remind me to send Bryce a bottle of—does anyone know what he drinks?" Deb asked the group at large.

"Bourbon," Luciano answered shortly, shooting Frankie an unamused look at her snort of laughter.

"Luc doesn't drink bourbon anymore after the last time

they drank together." She giggled. "I believe Bryce broke him as far as that particular drink is concerned."

"Querida, I told you that in confidence," Luciano grumbled. "I believe you will need to think of a way to make it up to me."

"I might have something in mind that will interest you," she saucily replied, biting her lip as she looked at him. Luciano's eyes darkened, his gaze riveted to her mouth.

Feeling an intruder to the intimate closeness between her friends, she glanced over to Mitch. He returned her gaze, unblinking, a deep yearning in his eyes.

Luciano stood. "I am glad you and the bebe are safe, Deb. Mitch, I was proud to stand with you today." He offered a firm hand to Mitch. "Now, I need to get my woman home before she tells all my secrets."

The love between them was obvious as Deb bid her friends farewell. She found herself envious of the strong bond they shared, a future they were forging entwined together.

Unbidden, a great rush of all the tension and emotions that had built up over the last few days gushed from her. Great heaving sobs shook her body, the release cathodic. Then, he was there. His strong arms wordlessly promised all would be okay. Through the haze of tears, his beloved face came into focus.

"I can't believe it. I'm finally free of him."

He lovingly wiped the tears from her eyes, his touch tender. "I promised you I'd never let anyone hurt you again and I meant every word of it. In fact, I'm almost thinking that this might turn into a full-time job for a bloke." He dropped down to one knee. "That is, if you'll let me." In his hand, he held an opal ring. "Deb, I keep telling you how much I love you and I love that little girl. It would make me the happiest bloke this side of the black stump if you would marry me."

Deb's heart overflowed as she gazed at the cowboy she

loved, the man who had, she now realized, always had her back and always would. "I hope you know what you're getting yourself into."

"Is that a yes?"

"With everything I have, yes." The last word had barely left her lips before Mitch leapt to his feet, knocking both of them over. Deb landed safely on Mitch, before he rolled her onto her back. He adoringly brushed the hair from her face.

"Well, my first job as your official fiancé is to make sure you're kissed at least ten times a day."

"Only ten times?" Deb teasingly protested.

"Oh, that's the bare minimum, I promise." He gazed into her eyes, passion stoking a fire inside her belly. "And I always keep my promises."

He lowered his face until his lips touched hers, his love flowing through the caress of his skin touching hers. As Deb closed her eyes and she lost herself to the sensation, she realized her cowboy had finally done it.

He had captured her cowgirl's heart.

EPILOGUE

Held within Mitch's strong embrace as they swayed together, Deb felt deliciously, completely, and utterly loved. "Are you happy, Deb?" he asked solicitously, love shining rapturously in his gaze.

He waited expectantly as she mulled her answer over. "I used to think love is what you found in fairy tales, but love isn't a feeling of bliss or constant butterflies. It's more a feeling that, no matter what happens, you have someone who has your back. It's unconditional. A couple of weeks into falling in love, it feels like Christmas morning. A couple of months into love feels like time has stopped. And a couple of years into love, it feels like home." She stroked his face tenderly as they danced. "And make no mistake, Mitch Eddison. I've loved you since kindy. I was just too blind to see it."

"So, is that a yes, then?" he teased, "I reckon it feels like a yes."

She gave his shoulder a gentle little tap. "It's a yes."

"Then, give your husband a kiss," he commanded.

Deb happily obeyed, the look in his eyes taking her breath away as the kiss ended. He stepped back, breaking the contact between them. Deb raised her eyebrow at him in question. Mitch simply smiled and crooked his finger, gesturing for her to follow. She curiously complied as he walked across the dancefloor to Sra Ana, Grace on her knee. He knelt down before them, his face level with the little girl.

"Gracie, can Daddy have the honor of this first dance with you and Mommy?" Deb's heart swelled so much that, for a moment, she couldn't feel anything except love for this wonderful man.

Her smile turned watery as Grace smiled and waved happily at Mitch. "Reckon a bloke can take that as a yes." He scooped Grace up in one strong arm, the other wrapped around Deb's waist, and led them back to the dancefloor.

Frankie, Gabi and Megan stood together. "Is that just the most precious thing you've ever seen?" Frankie blubbered. Megan silently offered a packet of tissues to her, then passed it to Gabi before discreetly dabbing at her own eyes. She wordlessly raised her glass to her friend in salute at her happiness.

After a final twirl, the newlyweds broke apart, Grace still ensconced in her daddy's arms. "It's time for all the single ladies to come to the dancefloor to catch the bouquet!" Deb excitedly announced.

Megan drained her glass and stepped determinedly onto the floor. Gabi remained resolutely beside Frankie. "She means you too, Gabriella," Sra Ana called from the side of the room. Gabi rolled her eyes, but obediently trotted out to join the others, already gathered.

Mitch, having retreated from the floor, found Luciano, Joao and Bryce in front of the dessert table. "I'm glad you were able to make it," he said, offering his hand to Bryce.

"It's my pleasure. And now I can finally try some of this famous pavlova Luciano is always bragging about his Querida making."

Mitch laughed. "Thanks again for everything you did with helping Deb."

"Don't mention it. I just gave Gabi some contacts. Anyway, can ya'll imagine what that gal would have done to me if I hadn't helped?" He shuddered in mock horror at the thought. "That just doesn't bear thinking about." He pulled a small silver hip flask from his coat pocket and took a sip as if to wash the disturbing thought from his mind.

The men watched as the women out on the floor began to jostle for position while Deb turned her back in preparation to throw the all-important bouquet. A flash of flowers shot high in the air, the technicolor sea of gowns swirling like currents in the ocean as they surged forward and one triumphant hand closed around the prize. The crowd parted to reveal the owner of the hand—Gabi.

Bryce wordlessly handed the flask to Joao. Luciano, laughing raucously, slapped him on the back in congratulations.

Out on the dancefloor, calm had been restored and, once again, Mitch, Deb and Grace had returned to their own private world. "Both of my girls look beautiful tonight," he said, a suspicious moisture in his eyes. "I might possibly be the luckiest bloke in the world to have such a good-looking family."

Family. The word struck a chord in Deb's soul. The three of them were a family, the very center of each other's universe. But it was more than that. They were lucky to be part of something bigger. She looked over to her friends and realized she had found what she had never known she was looking for. And the kicker? She'd had it all along. These people in this room, they were her family. She was home. She felt it in her cowgirl's heart, now and forever.

The End

As an Indie Author, reviews help me get my books noticed. If you enjoyed reading Deb's story as much as I did writing it, please leave a review, it will make all the difference to me

If you loved, *A Cowgirl's Heart,* sign up for my newsletter to get free bonus chapters from Frankie's wedding and bonus prequel as well as updates on new releases and exclusive extras.

Now, turn the page as the Affinity Stud Ranch story continues with Gabi…

A COWGIRL'S PASSION - SNEAK PEEK

Gabi paced in the aisle, her frenetic nervous energy frothing inside her, bubbling to the surface. It was this very same jitteriness that kept her muscles taut, as if perpetually ready for flight as she restlessly moved.

"You should sit down," Joao calmly suggested, his eyes glued to the giant screen as it flashed up the contestants that were next to run. "There are still five more to go till Frankie." He gave her a small, sideways smile. "Besides, Luciano will have finished his pep talk and will be out here with us before she runs."

Gabi grudgingly sat beside him, her foot twitching. Joao looked at it and then back up to her face, his lips quivering as he tried to suppress his laughter. "Don't you dare laugh at me, Joao Rojas!" she demanded, forcing her limb to be still. "I swear I don't know why Frankie was so excited that you guys could make it to see her ride. It's just more aggravation, if you ask me."

"I have not seen you nervous since you stopped wearing pig tails. It always seemed cute to me." He cast dark, laughing eyes at her. "I sometimes wish that maybe you'd wear them again."

Gabi's scathing retort died on her lips when she spotted Luciano making his way toward them. Jumping from her seat, she pushed past several disapproving spectators in her haste to get to him. She grabbed his arm. "Is she ready? How did she say Sampson felt? Maybe I should head back and see if she needs anything."

Luciano laughed, his eyes crinkling as he put his arm around her and forcibly returned her to her place. "How long has she been like this?" he asked the grinning Joao.

"Long enough that I worry she might cramp up from the pacing. I have tried to keep her hydrated."

Gabi let an exasperated sigh. "Are you going to tell me how she is or not, Luciano?"

"She is focused. Sampson looks good. They are ready. Now, we must do our bit and wait." He gave her an encouraging smile.

She nervously nibbled at her nail, giving a start of pain when she realized that she had bitten it down to the quick. Joao reached out and gently removed it from her mouth. Gabi gave him an irritated glare in return.

"She's next," Luciano said, leaning forward in anticipation, his gaze intent on the arena.

Gabi edged forward in her seat, unconsciously mirroring him. Luciano was right, even from the crowd you could see the look of determination on Frankie's face as Sampson barreled down the chute. The girl was taking no prisoners as she guided the gleaming ebony horse around the first drum, his muscles rippling beneath his onyx hide. Horse and rider moved as one as they flew across the sand like a laser-guided missile, intent on their target. The second and then the third barrels were clean, Sampson chasing down the finish line like he had the devil on his heels. The time flashed up. The fastest of the day. Gabi ecstatically bound to her feet, shrieking triumphantly.

"She did it! She's just qualified for the American Rodeo!"

Joao was on his feet beside her, Gabi only vaguely aware that Luciano was also standing and cheering. Without thinking, she grabbed Joao's face between her hands and planted a great, big, sloppy kiss on him. Gabi came jolting back to reality the moment she found herself staring into Joao's enormous, shocked eyes. Without a word, she released her hold on him and bolted from the stands, almost making as good a time as Sampson had moments earlier.

"Well, that's a first," a grinning Luciano noted. "But do the women you kiss, usually run away afterwards?"

"No, but maybe this one wants me to chase her?" Joao speculated, his eyes following her fleeing form.

"Maybe. But are you sure you want to catch her?"

"Yes. When I catch her, I will make sure she never wants me to let go." Joao said determination printed on his face.

Buy now on Amazon and Kindle Unlimited

ACKNOWLEDGMENTS

A debt of gratitude to my editor Rebekah Groves for her continued patience with me.

Another big thanks to Megan from Designed with Grace for her cover design. Still keeping the faith that we will eventually strike the motherlode for shirt clad cowboys

ABOUT THE AUTHOR

Edith MacKenzie or Eddie Mac to her friends is an author of sweet and wholesome contemporary cowboy romance. They say in literary circles to write what you know, and Eddie has certainly taken that to heart. Before embarking on a writing career, she trained horses professionally and brings that wealth of knowledge to her writing.

Now a mum to a boy and girl, as well as wife, she delights with her tales of strong cowgirls and their adventures in finding love. When not weaving the love stories of her characters, she enjoys hanging out with her family and animals, as well as reading, fishing and camping.

Just remember—once a cowgirl, always a cowgirl.